Sano's Queen

A NOVELLA

DARIE MCCOY

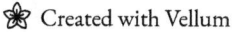 Created with Vellum

For my bestie, LDW. My life-long friend and confidant. Kari exists because of you.

Acknowledgments

This author journey has been a tremendous learning experience for me. It's a journey that I am grateful to take. My most sincere thanks to each author, reader and supporter who has been with me and offered me any form of guidance and encouragement. From the readers who generously reviewed my first novel and got in my inbox to ask about the next book to my sprint writing partners, I've received an abundance of blessings for which I am eternally grateful.

Author's Note

This novella was originally written as a part of anthology surrounding the 2020 Olympics. When the pandemic occurred, the Olympic games were postponed and when they resumed the games, there were a vast differences from the games in the past. When I decided to expand the novella from its original form, I made the conscious decision not to include the pandemic in any of my stories. As such, the timing wasn't changed from 2020 and any pandemic related concessions were not written into the story. I ask that the reader keep that in mind as they read this novella.

Prologue

"Another three pointer from Frost!"

The sports announcer yelled excitedly, turning to her co-commentator.

"The Queen is in a zone. She is playing like she has ice water in her veins. The Monarchs are in trouble if she keeps this up. "

The crowd roared following a turnover from the Monarch's center, which resulted in another three pointer from Frost. The lead referee issued a sharp whistle, signaling a time out on behalf of the Monarchs.

"Emily, someone check the weather report. I believe a cold front has descended on this arena. Frost has frozen the Monarch's defense. They **Do Not** have an answer for her."

"You're right Maria. If they don't get a handle on Frost, the second half of this game is going to result in an all-out slaughter."

Emily Sands watched the playback on the monitor along with Maria Carpenter.

"We knew this finals match-up would be tough. We've seen evidence of how evenly matched they are with the two trading victories leading to a winner-take-all situation in this final game of the seven game series."

The teams broke away from their respective huddles following the harsh blast of the horn, noting the end of the timeout. They then go on to spend the majority of the second half of the game in a back-and-forth battle resulting in the Fantasy holding on to a small lead well into the fourth quarter.

"Okay, Maria. We have a little over a minute left in the game and the Monarchs have just taken one of their two remaining time-outs. These players are leaving it all on the court. Both teams have played clean, but aggressive basketball. The Fantasy still holds the lead by six points, but with the time remaining on the clock, such a small margin doesn't guarantee them a win."

After Emily issued her sage commentary, the two continued their analysis of the game and possible opportunities the Monarchs had to increase their chances of at least sending the game into overtime.

The horn blast brought both teams back to the court. The rumble of the crowd was deafening, and the announcers were practically yelling into their headsets in order to be heard over the noise.

"Emily, the Monarch defense is really pressing the Fantasy hoping to cause a turnover. They need to be careful here. They have to play smart, but they can't allow too much time to pass with the ball in the hands of the Fantasy—especially with the way the Queen has been playing tonight."

"I agree Maria. Let's see how they play this."

Emily moves into a play-by-play analysis. Everything seemed to move in slow motion from that moment. Receiving the pass from her teammate, Kari Frost cuts right, trying to shake her defender. The defender bounces off the screen set by the Fantasy center giving Kari the space she needs to launch into the air releasing her patented jumper from just behind the three-point arc.

The announcer's faces morphed from excited enjoyment of basketball excellence to horror-stricken as they helplessly watched the scene unfold in front of them. The crowd went from screams of celebration, to deathly quiet. In the aftermath, two players lay on the floor—each writhing in pain.

Speaking softly into her headset, Maria described what was taking place on the court.

"Folks, if you are just joining us, we are live at MegaTech arena for game seven of the WNBA finals between the Los Angeles Monarchs and the Atlanta Fantasy. We have two injured players on the court and twenty seconds remaining in the game. The injured players are Sylvia Phillips from the Monarchs and Kari Frost from the Fantasy."

Emily interjected, "Phillips looks more stunned than injured, but Frost is being cared for by Dr. Daisuke Sano. It appears the Fantasy's team doctor Vincent Cotton is going to examine Frost right on the court... No, I take that back. Dr. Sano has intervened, and is taking her to the locker room."

"The Fantasy should thank their lucky stars Dr. Sano was in the building tonight. For those who don't know, he's the team physician for the NBA Champion Atlanta Harriers. He's helped many members of that particular team and other professional athletes recover from injuries which could have been career ending," Maria supplied.

Using their wealth of knowledge and experience, the two sports analysts broke down the play leading to the athletes lying on the floor.

Chapter One

KARI

"Shhh... *Kichōna*. I've got you."

Kari grasped the shoulders of the muscular man who hefted her from the floor. His inky, shoulder length hair brushed against her forehead and his voice was in her ear offering her words of comfort and strength as she tucked her head into the space below his chin. Vaguely, she could hear her teammates trying to get someone to tell them what was going on. Kari didn't know what was happening. All she knew for certain was the pain radiating from her knee wasn't good.

Dr. Sano was carrying her into the locker room, *actually carrying her* in his arms, and she wasn't even in a frame of mind to enjoy it. Instead, she focused all of her energy into making a graceful exit, trying to block out the excruciating pain in her knee that made her want to bawl like a newborn baby. The sheer magnitude of the pain made thoughts of much else almost impossible. Lifting her head from his broad shoulder, she gave a tight smile and wave to the crowd as she was transported from the court.

Even with the discomfort from her injury, she appreciated the warmth of Dr. Sano's body while he cradled her to his chest. None of their previous interactions had brought them in such close physical proximity. With his handsome Japanese features, his face, set in stern lines, and hardened glint of his brown almond shaped eyes, he acted as a deterrent to anyone who approached them on their route to the locker room. His powerful aura seemed to insulate them from everyone around.

A sharp hiss escaped her lips when he laid her gently on the padded table located in the anterior of the locker room area. Making comforting shushing noises, he carefully arranged her legs on the table to begin his examination.

"Dr. Sano, I appreciate the assistance, but I can take it from here."

Dr. Vincent Cotton's nasally voice cut through the comfortable silence between Kari and Dr. Sano. Dr. Cotton took a position on the right side of the table. When he stretched his hand over Kari's right leg, preparing to start his own examination, the gravelly voice of J. Daisuke Sano gave him pause.

"Do not touch her," Dr. Sano growled at the other man.

Kari's eyes widened and flew to his face. His visage was set in hard, menacing lines. It was well known the two weren't friendly, but up until now, they had always been professional.

His entire demeanor screamed badass. In the past, Kari had mostly ever seen Dr. Sano exhibit warmth and friendliness. He was nothing like the stereotypical images of overly stern Japanese men which were still so pervasive in movies. Granted, he could be a little intense when she came back to the bench after getting into a scrape with another player. As a very physical player, random scratches and scrapes were inevitable.

Technically, as the Fantasy's team physician, Dr. Cotton should have been the one to oversee Kari's care, but Dr. Sano blocked Cotton's attempts to perform his duties. Sano was the first to reach Kari when she fell to the court. He was the one who asked her the initial questions in order to make a quick assessment of her condition and determine the best way to proceed.

It was also Dr. Sano who told her coach, point blank, she was done for the night and he was taking her to the locker room. It was his calmness and comfort which held her together until she made it away from the arena and could allow her tears to flow freely.

Glaring at Dr. Sano, Dr. Cotton blustered, "Listen here –"

"Gentlemen! We don't have time for this. Dr. Cotton, step back and let Dr. Sano work," Sonia Miller's voice sliced into the discussion—heading off the brewing confrontation between the physicians.

Following the orders from the head coach, Dr. Cotton sealed his lips —not daring to go against her.

Craning her neck, to peek around Dr. Sano's bulky frame at Coach Miller, Kari asked, "Coach, what are you doing in here? The game's still going on."

"Why don't you let me worry about the game, and you concentrate on doing what Dr. Sano says so we can get an idea of what's going on with your knee?"

Coach Miller brushed off Kari's concerns.

"Besides, I left McAdams in charge. With your last three pointer, we're up by six again. Ref called a foul on Phillips. Gayden is taking the free throws, so you can count the baskets as a gimme. I'm confident we can hold them off for another twenty seconds of play."

Just as the coach made her statement, thunderous cheers shook the arena. A broad grin graced her face as she patted Kari's shoulder, "See. I told you. What you're hearing is the sound of a championship win."

"My queen, I need your attention now," Dr. Sano said in his low, rumbling voice.

In spite of the situation, Kari's stomach fluttered when he called her *his* queen. She should be used to it by now, since he'd addressed her that way from the moment he joined the Harriers' staff almost a year ago. Usually, he combined his words with a reverent bow of his head. This time, his eyes held hers captive until she gave him a curt nod.

She'd long ago convinced herself he didn't mean it as a term of endearment. Picking it up from her teammates, he was just taking the nickname a bit further. It was their inside joke. *Right?* He wasn't actually saying she was **his**. *Nah...*

While Dr. Cotton stood against the wall, silently fuming, Dr. Sano lifted her uninjured left leg, with a hand in the bend of her leg behind the knee. He pressed her lower leg forward testing the range of motion and behavior of the kneecap and tibia. Having watched other players be examined in the past helped Kari recognize and understand his actions. He was checking the ACL (Anterior Cruciate Ligament) of her uninjured leg so he would have a reference point for comparison to her injured limb.

It was hard not to note the differences of approach between the two physicians. Were it left to Cotton, he would have examined the injured leg without first testing the uninjured leg to get an idea of how her knee behaved when there wasn't a potentially torn ligament.

Lying quietly, she closed her eyes while Dr. Sano took her uninjured limb through his series of tests. Anxiety caused her thoughts to race and her pulse to quicken. If her ACL was torn, it could mean the end of her career as a professional basketball player. Every professional athlete knew someone who'd had surgery and recovered from ACL injuries, but she was acutely aware of the statistics.

The ability to recover from a torn ACL hinged on many factors, which included adequate time to rest and rehab the injury as well as the age and activity level of the individual. Kari was approaching her mid-thirties. The plan was to play one more season before retiring. A torn ACL would mean she had most likely played her last game as a member of the *Fantasy*. Anyone with knowledge of ACL injuries knew the athlete *never* regained full use of the knee following such a wound.

To add to her concern was the possibility of her position being jeopardized as a member of Team USA Women's Basketball. *What if it really is my ACL? What if it's completely torn?*

Thoughts of her Olympic and professional careers ending in one fell swoop caused her vision to blur and tears to leak from her eyes. If her last act as a professional athlete was to help her team secure another championship she would be proud, but she'd much rather finish her career on her own terms.

~

JONATHAN DAISUKE SANO

Daisuke focused one hundred percent of his attention on Kari. As soon as the other man took a step back from the table and Daisuke was assured only he would oversee the care of his *Kichōna*, he'd dismissed Cotton from his mind.

Gratitude pulsed through him in thankfulness for every string he'd pulled to make certain he was courtside for every *Fantasy* home game. If Kari suffered an injury and he wasn't present to make sure she was handled correctly, he wouldn't be able to forgive himself. *Was this normal? No. Did he care how it looked? Also, no.*

Beyond minor scratches and bruises, he didn't trust Cotton with dispensing medical treatment. *Someone else's* scratches and bruises, not Kari's. From the moment he'd met her, Daisuke decided he would be the only one to take care of her needs.

He had yet to act on his instant attraction to her romantically, but he made sure he was present whenever possible to watch over her. Without being a complete stalker, he ensured he had opportunities for the two of them to hold conversations which weren't necessarily centered on sports. He'd wanted to spend time really getting to know her before venturing into intimacy. For now, he claimed domain over her athletic health.

With an unreadable expression on his face, Daisuke finished his initial examination. He had some thoughts on the severity of Kari's injury but wanted scans to be certain of the diagnosis. He also wanted to consult with his partners on the case. As much as he wanted and planned to be involved in her treatment and recovery, he knew he was too close to be completely objective. What he needed was the discernment and experience of physicians he could trust.

Lifting his eyes to Kari's tear-streaked face, he called upon the strength and discipline of his Samurai ancestors to stay the instinct to demand everyone leave the room so he could gather his *Kichōna* into his arms and comfort her.

His control only extended so far. He couldn't restrain his hand, which reached to cup the side of her face—fingers extending into her wild curls, one thumb wiping away the thin trail of tears from her temple. Her eyes were hidden behind tightly closed lids.

"Shhh... *Shi no shin*," He murmured to her softly.

In an obvious attempt to contain her emotions, her right hand gripped her uniform shorts. Her left hand was fisted on her stomach, clenching her jersey. Prompting her to open her eyes, Daisuke covered her left hand and gave it a gentle squeeze. Leaning over her prone frame, he peered into her hazel-brown orbs attempting to transfer his strength to her through their locked stare. Releasing her fist, she turned her hand to tangle her fingers with his, before giving him another slight nod of the head.

Freeing Kari from his intense gaze, he focused on Coach Miller. He appreciated her confidence in him above her own team physician. It wasn't hard to hear the noise from the arena and he knew at any moment the inner doors to the locker room could bang open allowing the celebratory team entry into the area.

"Coach Miller, I know you are anxious to hear my assessment. However, I would prefer to take her to my facility for further scans. Then, I will discuss her condition with her and whomever she chooses to inform after we speak." Daisuke issued his statement, still maintaining physical contact with Kari.

Coach Miller visibly stiffened, but didn't contradict his request. She transferred her full attention to Kari.

"Is that how you want to handle this, Queen?"

Miller placed the choice where it belonged—with her point guard. Feeling the quick squeeze and release of his fingers, Daisuke fixed his eyes back on Kari's tear-stained face.

The tug he felt was her trying to sit up on the table. As she rose to a sitting position, her gaze moved between him and the coach, her face a mask of determination with a tinge of apprehension. When she spoke her voice was soft, but clear.

"Can I at least do the post-game before we leave? I mean, can't we wrap and ice my knee? I could use some crutches or a chair until after. Then, we can go get the scans when we're done. If this is going to be my last time, I don't want to miss this. I want to be here for my teammates."

"I never said your injury would keep you from playing again," Daisuke said in a chiding tone. He didn't want to give her false hope, but he also didn't want her thinking so negatively about her injury.

"I know, but it could be. Right?" Kari captured his eyes, silently pleading with him.

Her request was reasonable, and completely possible, but Daisuke battled internally to prevent himself from whisking her away. It went against everything in him to leave her in pain for a second longer than necessary. He buckled under the weight of her earnest request and pleading eyes.

The table on which she lay was in the area designated for tending to a player's medical needs. Scanning the shelves for what he needed, he proceeded to quickly stabilize her injured knee with a temporary brace and attached cool packs to the wrapping to keep the swelling down. Instead of administering a pain-relieving cortisone shot, he pressed two extra strength aspirin into her hand and coaxed her to take them with a bottle of water.

Once he was done, Kari gifted him with a watery smile to express her thanks. Moments later, the doors burst open; the inner and outer areas of the locker room were flooded with Fantasy team members and staff chattering excitedly.

Helping Kari from the table, Daisuke held out a set of crutches. Proving she was no stranger to using crutches, she took hold of the walking aids. After a brief pause to allow him to adjust them to suit her 5'-9" height, she positioned them against her torso and ventured into the fray.

Despite the care he noted her teammates used with her, he remained close by ready to jump to her assistance at the first sign she needed him. He refused to examine his overprotective actions and didn't give a rat's ass that Cotton remained nearby as well. Daisuke was done being on the sidelines of Kari's life.

Chapter Two

DAISUKE

Daisuke allowed Kari exactly an hour to celebrate with her team and participate in post-game interviews before gently, but firmly, prompting her to gather her belongings and guided her from the arena.

While he waited for her to finish celebrating with her team, he'd called his partners and arranged for the ambulance service onsite to transport her to the complex in which his practice and rehabilitation facility, HJR, was housed. Opting to ride along in the ambulance, he left his vehicle at the arena.

During the drive over to the complex Kari split her time between talking softly on her phone and texting someone. *Who the fuck is she texting? Why is she talking so softly?* Even though the questions raced through his head, he held back from demanding to know who was on the other end of the calls and texts. Officially, he wasn't in the position to question her about the people in her life. He clenched his jaw and kept his thoughts to himself. For the moment.

Mere minutes after they arrived at the facility, a dark SUV pulled into a space alongside the ambulance. Keeping one eye on the paramedics removing Kari from the ambulance, he observed the four people who exited the SUV.

He recognized Kari's parents, Archer and Tami Frost. Archer stood tall beside his wife, his slender, but muscular body tense with worry. Sharp, concerned-filled blue eyes watched Kari intently. Tami was the parent who gifted Kari with the smooth brown skin and curvy hips that had been the source of many of Daisuke's fantasies. Taller than her mother and shorter than her father, Kari was the perfect mixture of the two in her features.

He'd seen and spoken to her parents countless times at the *Fantasy* home games. Since he had every intention of being a part of Kari's life, he interacted with her parents in order to get to know them as well. *That was totally not weird. Nope. Not a bit.*

Vaguely, he remembered the other couple from a few games they'd attended. He was positive the other couple were her aunt and uncle. There was no mistaking Kari's uncle Drew. He was an almost exact duplicate of her father—with a different haircut. After quick introductions, Daisuke ushered everyone inside the building.

Dr. Raphael Mitchell and Dr. Henry Williams arrived just as he was finishing the preparations with Kari for an MRI. Daisuke turned from the imaging station to greet his partners.

The three had met in medical school. Hanging out in med school their eclectic Asian, Hispanic, African-American ensemble, when mentioned, sounded like the beginning of a tasteless joke—a Black man, Asian man and a Mexican walk into a bar...

"Raph, Henry. Thank you for coming in on a Saturday evening."

Daisuke walked the two over to the imaging table to meet Kari.

"My queen, I'd like you to meet Doctors Raphael Mitchell and Henry Williams. They are my partners. Dr. Mitchell is a Radiologic specialist and Dr. Williams specializes in Kinesiology and Physical Therapy. They will assist with your diagnosis and determining our best course of action for treatment."

"My queen?"

Raphael repeated. Lifting his eyebrows in surprise, his eyes bounced between Daisuke and Kari.

With a hand flip in Daisuke's direction, Kari responded to his questioning tone, "Don't mind him. It's a running joke because people call me *Queen* as a nickname."

Daisuke stiffened under the comment but didn't challenge her explanation. Obviously, she didn't know he was **never** joking when he called her *his queen*. She would learn that soon enough. He knew her teammates called her 'Queen', because she was crowned Homecoming Queen in both High School and College. It suited her, but not for the reasons others used it.

The two men each offered Kari brief, professional handshakes. Daisuke ignored the probing stare he received from Raphael. As his partner as well as his best friend, Raph was aware of his attraction to Kari. He knew his friend would have something to say about him forcing himself into overseeing her care.

By the time the scans were completed and he'd finished his consultation with Raphael, Coach Miller had joined Kari's family in the waiting area. Raphael had analyzed the scans and Henry had offered treatment suggestions.

From his position in the open doorway leading from the imaging area, Daisuke could see Kari's supporters gathered together in the spacious area at the front of the facility. Since it was the weekend, the small group were the only other people in the building—aside from the patrolling security guards.

While Daisuke rolled Kari into the hall in one of their spare wheelchairs, he asked Raphael to queue up the images in the consultation room.

"My queen, would you prefer a private consultation, or do you want your coach and family present?" Leaning in closely, he spoke directly into her ear.

"You can ask them all to come in. I'd rather they hear it directly from you instead of me having to explain it later." Kari responded, her voice sullen and resigned.

"Dr. Williams, would you mind escorting the people from the waiting area into the consultation room? I need to speak with my queen," Daisuke said to Henry.

Not liking the morose quality of her voice, he needed a moment to speak with his *Kichōna*. Pulling the brake handle to lock the wheels on the chair, he moved in front of her. Placing his hands on the back of the chair, he bracketed her shoulders.

His chocolate brown eyes captured hers, demanding her full attention.

"*Shi no shin,* you sound like you've already decided the news will be bad. You haven't seen the scans or heard the results; yet you seem like you've already given up. In all the time I've known you, I've never known you to be a quitter," he chided.

Her eyes skittered away from his intense gaze. Cupping her chin, he brought her focus back to his face.

"Now is the time for positive thoughts and attitude. Okay?"

Nothing.

She sat quietly in the chair. Almost mutinous in her silence. Tightening his hold on her chin, he asked.

"Do you need me to motivate you?"

He felt and saw her pulse quicken at his suggestion. Daisuke wondered if she imagined the ways in which he wanted to *motivate* her into a more positive attitude. Several, completely unprofessional, options came to his mind immediately. One option involved his open palm connecting with her luscious ass.

"Umm... That won't be necessary. I'm okay."

Kari finally answered following their short stare down. Searching her eyes a moment longer, he stood and rounded the chair. He set them in motion again, moving into the consultation room.

KARI

Kari sat in the special wheelchair keeping her leg elevated, because a full bend wasn't possible at the moment. After the MRI and X-rays, Dr. Sano wrapped and secured her knee in another brace. He wouldn't allow her to walk to the consulting room on the crutches she'd used before, so the chair was her only option.

Dr. Sano wheeled her to the head of the conference table and moved to the seat immediately to her right. There was an open laptop on the table in front of the empty seat he chose. Her family and Coach Miller were already seated.

Her Uncle Andrew and Aunt Bonita were at the game with her parents, so they were seated at the table as well. Concern was etched across the face of her very empathetic mother. Wondering if they knew something she didn't, Kari observed the tense expressions on the faces of her coach and family members.

"Are you okay, sweetie? Do you need anything?"

Her mother asked nervously, while she smoothed stray strands of hair back from Kari's face.

"I'm okay, Mama," Kari assured her.

It was a lie. She was **not** okay. She was terrified, anxious and completely on edge, but she wouldn't tell them anything of the kind. Her mother already looked to be on the verge of tears. Kari wasn't going to give her a reason to turn on the waterworks. She shared a very close relationship with her mom, so her mother knew how important basketball and competing in the Olympics were to her.

There was no way she could let on how deeply she was affected by the very thought of her career being over. Giving them the slightest inkling that she was thinking her career was over wasn't an option. She couldn't go down that road. If she allowed the idea too much room in her brain, she'd become a blubbering mess and her mom would join her.

Her mother was part Miccosukee (Seminole). Kari had boatloads of stories she'd been told as a child about her mom's *extra helping* of passion and emotion due to her being both African American and Miccosukee. *"Our people feel things very deeply,"* she often told Kari during her childhood.

No. Kari would hold it together. Dr. Sano was right. She didn't know for sure this was the end. *Don't manifest negativity in your life. Nothing is over until it's over.* Dr. Sano's chocolate pools were waiting for her when her eyes drifted to her right. If she believed in such things, she would think he was speaking to her telepathically. She could hear his words reverberating in her ears. *"Do you need me to motivate you?"*

Dropping her eyes to his hands resting on the table, she observed his long, thick fingers. Veins stood out on the back of his hands, hinting at the power they held. Shaking herself from her thoughts, she concentrated on the situation at hand. She so *did not* need to think of any of the ways in which she would be more than happy for him to use those strong hands to *motivate* her.

"What's the verdict Doc? Or is it Docs, since there are three of you?"

She asked in the most upbeat tone she could manage. Her smile watery, but present. Flitting her gaze between the three doctors, she waited for one of them to speak.

Speaking first, Dr. Sano asked, "Why don't we start with the good news?"

"Works for me. I could use more good news," Coach Miller smiled in an apparent attempt to help lighten the mood in the room.

Dr. Sano tapped a few keys on the laptop and clicked the mouse. The X-Ray and MRI images appeared in a tiled arrangement on the enormous television screens mounted on the wall.

Kari had seen similar images before. With her love of medical dramas, she'd learned enough to know she wouldn't have survived medical school, but she did recognize her femur, patella and tibia.

"My concern after my initial examination was a torn Anterior Cruciate Ligament or ACL. Drs. Mitchell and Williams agree this isn't a complete tear. That's the good news."

Dr. Sano swept his gaze around the room before returning to Kari's face. The way he watched her made her feel like he was trying to syphon the thoughts right out of her brain. It was either that, or he was trying the telepathy thing again.

A feeling of euphoria washed over Kari before his words completely settled. Her joy at hearing 'not torn' was dampened somewhat when the full weight of what he actually said penetrated the euphoric bubble.

Thinking of the way he phrased the sentence, she asked, "You said it's not a complete tear. Does that mean it's partially torn?" Her voice wavered toward the end of the sentence as her brain immediately fed her possible scenarios.

Clicking one image to enlarge it, Dr. Sano continued. "You have what is referred to as a Stage 2 sprain of the ACL."

Using the mouse to hover over a portion of the scans, he described her injury.

"In layman's terms, it just stretched almost to its limits, but it didn't separate from the bone completely. Because roughly ninety percent of the ligament is still attached, we don't think you will need to take the surgical route to recovery. We are recommending you stay off it for a few weeks. After a period of time to allow it to heal naturally, you can begin rehabilitation."

"How long would I have to rehab?"

While she was relieved to hear she wouldn't need surgery, she knew the rehabilitation process for ACL injuries could last months. Team USA had exhibition games scheduled during the fall and winter as part of the preparations for the 2020 Olympics.

If she couldn't be in playing condition by the time they began practicing, her chances of being one of the twenty players to make the trip to Tokyo would be almost nonexistent.

"The rehabilitation period depends on a few factors. You're already in great physical condition, so that will work in your favor. However, I will be straight with you. It could last at least three months," Dr. Sano issued the information in his normal straight forward manner.

Whether or not it was his intention, the deep timbre of his voice and his succinct speech pattern had a calming effect on her. She trusted him, and by extension, she trusted his partners. Nodding, she accepted his statement. Internal prayers of thanks were sent up—for her diagnosis and her family being present for moral support. Even though they were mostly silent, their presence was comforting.

Trying to infuse as much cheer as she could muster into her voice, she asked, "So what's next?"

Kari, Coach Miller, and her family listened attentively as Drs. Sano and Williams discussed treatment and rehabilitation options. It didn't escape her notice that Dr. Sano never mentioned Dr. Cotton, or any other physicians outside of his partners, having involvement in the plan.

Deciding not to analyze that too deeply, she pressed on. Dr. Cotton wasn't one of her favorite people anyway. He wasn't a creeper; he just didn't seem like he was equipped for sports medicine.

Following the consultation, Dr. Williams fitted her with a new set of crutches. They were ergonomic and adjusted to her height better than the loaner crutches from the arena medical pit. In addition to the crutches, he also assisted her with a better knee brace and walked her through the ins and outs of how the next few weeks would go while she healed.

All of this was done under the watchful eye of Daisuke Sano. Since his portion of the treatment was completed, Dr. Mitchell left following the consultation. He wouldn't be needed again until it was time to take progress scans on her knee.

When it was time to leave, her father assured Dr. Sano they could transport her since his SUV had three rows. Kari saw a fleeting look she thought might have been frustration flash across the doctor's face, but it was gone so quickly, she couldn't be sure.

Seeing as she wasn't able to climb into the back to sit on the third row, and her father and uncle were much too tall, her mom and Aunt Bonita pulled the short straws and clambered into the vehicle's third row of seats. Kari's father and uncle helped her into the back seat, taking care to support her knee and not bump it on the hard metal.

When she hazarded a glance at Dr. Sano, she saw him standing at the edge of the sidewalk. Hands stuffed into the pockets of his white coat, his mouth was set in a grim line. His posture screamed his tension in the situation. *Didn't he trust her own father to take care of her?*

Capturing his gaze, she offered him a tentative smile. "Thank you again Dr. Sano."

"Daisuke," He corrected her.

"Huh?" Her brow furrowed in question.

"You will call me Daisuke, my queen. And, you don't owe me any thanks. It's my job to take care of you," he informed her. His eyes boring into hers. Even though he wasn't close to her, his presence seemed massive.

"Umm... Okay... See you later then," Her voice rising at the end of her sentence, making it sound like a question.

"Yes, my queen. I'll see you soon," he said, stepping back farther from the vehicle.

Her parents, aunt and uncle remained conspicuously quiet throughout the exchange. As soon as her father pulled away from the parking space, her Aunt Bonita started the inquisition.

"So, what's up with you and the sexy Asian doctor? Why does he call you **his queen**? He was standing on the curb looking like he wanted to push Drew and Archer on the ground so he could snatch you up and take you home with him," her aunt delivered her statement in the way only her Aunt Bonita could get away with—brutally blunt.

Dropping her head to the seat rest, Kari closed her eyes. "Auntie..." This was going to be a long ride.

~

Monday

Knocks on the bathroom door interrupted Kari in the slow process of taking care of her basic hygiene needs. Immediately following the knocks, her mother's voice reached her through the closed door, "Kari, you have a phone call. It's that nice Dr. Sano."

Say what now? Snapping her head around so fast she almost lost her balance, Kari snapped out, "I'm sorry, what? There's a call for me from who?"

A closed door meant nothing to her mother. The knob on the door twisted in a testing manner, then was pushed open by her non-boundary-having mother.

"It's Dr. Sano. He's calling to check on you. Isn't that just the sweetest thing?"

Since when does Daisuke call me? This isn't real. I'm in an alternate reality, or something. We talk when we see each other. And I would definitely remember giving his fine ass my number. Numb fingers reached out to take the phone.

"Hello?"

Flowing through the device, Daisuke's smooth tenor entered her ear. "Good morning, *Kichōna*. How are you feeling?"

"Um... I'm managing."

Unsure how she was supposed to take the inquiry, she went with the truth. Ignoring her mom standing just outside the bathroom, ear hustling, Kari maneuvered on one crutch, making her way into her bedroom. Taking a seat on the ottoman at the foot of the bed, she fought against asking the questions rolling around in her head.

Questions like... Am I dreaming? How the hell did you get my number? Why are you calling me like it's normal?

20

It was completely against her nature to allow a man the kind of latitude she was giving him. Calling her without permission? Getting all up in her business? Nope. Doesn't happen.

That's invitation-only level. If you're not invited, you don't get in. But...It's *Daisuke*. He didn't know it, and if confronted, she'd deny it, but his overbearing behind could just about get whatever he wanted, whenever he wanted it. *So, what does he want?*

Accepting her vague answer about her well-being, he asked a few more questions and before she knew it, they were in the midst of a full-blown conversation. An *enjoyable* conversation. Eventually, her mom walked out of the bedroom, but she didn't stray far. Kari knew she was just lying in wait, listening, anticipating the chance to grill her about every detail.

Time slipped away from them, and they spent more than a half hour on the phone. Needing to get back to his scheduled patients, he ended the call with the promise of calling her later in the evening. Pressing the icon to end the call, she indulged in a silent scream. **Oh. My. God!**

Leaning over to peer out the open bedroom door, she called out, "Mama, you can quit pretending to water that plant. I'm off the phone."

Appearing in the doorway, one hand pressed against her chest, her mother's dark eyes were wide with fake shock, "What? This poor plant is at death's door. I'm trying to save it. I wasn't trying to eavesdrop on your little call with your sexy doctor man."

Giving her serious side eye, Kari pulled herself up on both crutches and hobbled from the room.

"Sure, Mama. Sure. Thanks for keeping my plant alive."

Settling herself on the sofa, she tapped out a text message to her bestie/cousin Candace.

Kari: Gurl! You will not believe what just happened!
Candy: What?
Kari: J. Daisuke Sano just called me!
Candy: Whaaaat?
Kari: Yes! You could have knocked me over with a feather.
Candy: I'm going to call you. I need the deets!

Kari: No! Mama's still here. I'll call you when she doesn't have her ears in my conversation.

Candy: You better not forget!

Kari: I won't.

Still somewhat shocked that Daisuke called her, she sat quietly trying to process it all. Replaying their conversation in her head. As thankful as she was to have her mother's help, she really wanted to speak freely to her bestie.

The way her mom hovered, it was unlikely she'd get any privacy until later. So, the moment her mama left for the night, she would be on the phone with Candy attempting to unpack this whole situation.

Chapter Three

KARI

One week later

"Queen! Where you at?"

Kelly White's voice reached Kari as she was finishing up in the bathroom.

"Give me a minute!"

Yelling back, she maneuvered on the crutches to flush the toilet and wash her hands. Exiting the restroom situated to the left of her living room, she found three of her teammates standing in her foyer. Kelly White, Terri Forest and Fredricka Gayden the starting Center, Power Forward and Two Guard each held a reusable shopping bag from the healthy grocery store nearby.

Giving her teammates a questioning look, Kari asked "How did y'all get in my house? I know my mom locked the door when she left."

"Is that any way to greet your teammates who came over to see about the sick and shut in?" Kelly joked.

"We even brought sustenance. We know how you like sustenance."

Terri added making a reference to one of the online comics Kari liked to follow on social media.

Fredricka supplied Kari with the answer to her question. "We pulled up as your mom was getting ready to leave. She let us in so you wouldn't have to get up to open the door."

Her mother had been at her house every day for the past week. If she and her father hadn't put their foot down, Kari knew her mom would have tried to force her to move in with them, or moved into her home with her, while she recovered.

Heck, if Kari's father hadn't called her home, the woman would still be here. Neither of them would tell her that Kari asked him to do it. There was no need to hurt her feelings. Kari just needed a little break from the hovering.

Moving into the living room, ignoring Kelly's sick and shut-in joke, she focused on the bags they carried.

"What did you bring me?" She asked, settling herself in the corner of her L-shaped couch.

Small mountains of pillows and blankets had been arranged in the area by her mother. The corner was filled with anything she thought would help Kari be comfortable.

Each of her teammates placed a bag next to her on the couch and Kelly answered her question.

"We just brought some kinda-healthy snack options for you. We all know what it's like being laid up. You've really got nothing to do but eat, sleep, watch TV and play on the internet. You can't exercise, or move around too much, so everything you eat goes directly to your ass."

Turning to the side with her hip pushed out, Fredricka gave her butt a light pop.

"Ain't nothing wrong with a little junk in the trunk. Gotta give your boo something to hold on to, *or smack*," she grinned, holding one hand out in front of her while she made a swatting motion with the other hand.

Kelly cocked an eyebrow at Fredricka's antics.

"Little girl, if you don't get yourself somewhere."

The laughter tumbling from her own mouth ruined Kelly's attempt to reprimand her younger teammate for her playful nature. Their laughter was contagious, drawing Kari and Terri in.

"Thanks for the giggles *and* the snacks. Y'all didn't have to bring me anything, though. Please have a seat."

Finally remembering her manners, Kari extended the invitation. While she rooted around in the bags, her teammates took seats around the room.

Leaning over, Terri looked more closely at the colorful bouquet of flowers on the side table next to her. When she started gently probing between the flowers, Kari cocked an eyebrow at her.

"Ma'am. Exactly what are you doing?"

Even though she had a good idea what Terri was doing, she asked anyway. Terri was looking for the card that was supposed to be mixed in with the flowers.

"Don't play crazy. I'm looking for the card to these flowers. Where is it? Who sent these?" Terri asked.

The bouquet next to her was one of four flower arrangements around the room. The arrangement in question consisted of red camellias, daffodils and white heather. It was beautiful and fragrant.

Terri leaned in sniffing the aromatic blossoms. "Whoever sent them has good taste. They look and smell wonderful."

"I bet I know who they're from," Kelly said, wiggling her eyebrows and shimmy shaking her shoulders.

"Mind your business. It doesn't matter who sent them. For all you know, they could be from Coach," Kari said attempting to put them off. *They are so nosey!*

"Wait. Don't red camellias mean something about being a flame in someone's heart and daffodils are like something about being someone's sunshine? Or something like that?" Fredricka asked.

Three pairs of eyes swung around to her face in response to her statement.

"What?" She hunched her shoulders. "My favorite aunt owns a flower shop. I spent a lot of time there growing up."

"Annnywaay..." Kelly dragged the word out, turning her attention back to Kari. "You don't have to tell us, because I know for sure now who sent them."

Crossing her arms, Kari pinned her gaze on Kelly. "Since you know everything, who sent them?"

"**Sexy Sano** sent all of these flowers except the bouquet over there on the bar. That one came from the team. I know, because I picked out the arrangement," Kelly supplied smugly.

Leaning back in the chair, she stretched her long legs out in front of her crossing them at the ankle.

"Ugh! You make me sick! Why do you have to be right all the time? And please stop calling Daisuke *Sexy Sano,*" Kari pouted.

There really was no reason for her to be upset, but she wasn't sure what to make of Daisuke's attention; so, she wasn't ready to share *any* details with them yet.

From the moment she began her mandated rest period, Daisuke had been attentive to her in different ways. First, he'd sent her flowers four out of the seven days, starting the Monday after her injury. On top of the flowers, he also called her twice daily to check on her.

Only her mom and Candy knew about the flowers and the phone calls. The only reason her mom knew was because she was there at her home when both the deliveries and calls occurred. Otherwise, Kari would have only shared it with Candy. Now her teammates knew about the flowers, but she had no plans to tell them about the calls.

"Don't try to act brand new. You know we've been calling him Sexy Sano from day one. Why should we change now?"

Terri was right, but Kari didn't want to hear logic at the moment.

"Exactly," Kelly co-signed Terri's statement.

Waving a hand over the length of her six foot-seven inch frame, she emphasized her impressive height.

"Cause, for real for real. If I thought he was remotely interested in me, I'd let him climb the tree that is me in a heartbeat,"

Kari rolled her eyes at Kelly's declaration. In the past week, her own crush on Daisuke had grown into something different. She was unwilling to put a name on it, but from their first phone conversation she began to think of him as much more than the doctor she fantasized about. More than the man who chatted with her around the practice facility and who was always there to patch her scrapes during home games.

Trying a different approach, Kari snipped, "I never called him Sexy Sano—y'all did. Anyway... Kelly, how are you so sure he sent the flowers?"

With skepticism written all over her face, Kelly flipped her long ponytail over her shoulder and leaned forward, pinning Kari with her sharp gaze.

"Pfft! Please, honey. Don't sit over there pretending you didn't know that man is into you. First of all, he calls you *My Queen*, instead of just *Queen* like the rest of us. Second, he practically pushes poor Dr. Cotton out of the way any time you get so much as a scratch. There's no way you didn't know he was feeling you."

"What? He calls me *'My Queen'* as a joke! And he doesn't push Dr. Cotton to the side,"

Kari was quick to deny Kelly's words, but her mind was replaying random memories from the past year. In each flash, Daisuke's face was fixed with concern as he applied ointments and bandages to any minor abrasion she received during the game.

There's no way he's been into me all this time and I missed it. Candy said I was being deliberately obtuse, but she wasn't around much to see everything firsthand. Nope! I refuse to believe he was feeling me and I didn't catch on. That's my story and I'm sticking to it.

"Woman please! You're the only one who thinks it's a joke."

Tossing her head, Terri's strawberry blonde hair whipped back from her lightly freckled face.

"Poor Dr. Cotton. If he even looked like he wanted to touch you, Sano would give him the evil eye. The man isn't even our team doctor and he is at **ev-e-ry** home game, sitting at the end of the bench like he was supposed to be there. And we're not going to talk about the fact that he **never** intervenes when Dr. Cotton treats anyone else on the team."

"That's not true! When Wendy broke her finger, he was the one who set it and taped it for her," Kari hastily challenged Terri's statement.

"One time. In the entire year he's been hanging around, he's treated someone else on the team exactly one time," Kelly said. "That never struck you as odd? You are not even close to being that oblivious. You can tell that lie to somebody else." Pointing a finger at Kari, Kelly continued, "**You** watch everything and everyone."

Not to be left out, Fredricka added her two cents.

"For real though. When you hit the floor holding your knee, I don't think he even waited for the whistle. Before I even realized anything was wrong, he was already next to you on the court."

"Face it, girlfriend. The man is seriously into you. I don't know what your deal is—why you're trying to pretend there's nothing there. But, it's past time you two stop playing around and do something about it. If you ask me, I'd say Sexy Sano is making his move."

Kelly added her advice with a pointed look at the flowers on the different surfaces around the room.

Kari really wasn't in the mood to delve into her feelings about Daisuke or speculate on how he felt about her.

"Moving on," she said in a not-so-subtle attempt to change the subject.

"Have y'all heard anything else about the rest of the events lined up to celebrate the championship? I've got to figure out what to wear with this brace and crutches. I also need to get an appointment with Steph to do something to my hair. Freddy, you're our fashionista. Any ideas for brace and crutch friendly attire?"

Kari hoped Fredricka would be true to form and take the bait, and her younger teammate didn't let her down. Bringing up clothes, hair and a party was a sure-fire way to get Fredricka going.

Contrary to outdated opinions about female athletes, they are just as feminine as other women and many of them enjoy opportunities to completely glam it up, wearing pretty outfits, and cute shoes.

Fredricka's enthusiasm was infectious, and she soon pulled Terri and Kelly into the discussion about the upcoming celebratory events. With the discussion turned away from Daisuke, Kari sat back in her seat and enjoyed the remainder of her visit with her teammates.

~

DAISUKE

Two weeks later

She's here. The tingling in his spine alerted Daisuke to Kari's presence. The spinal tingling was his early warning system, since it only occurred when she was nearby. He'd just finished with his last patient of the day. Knowing today was her first day of rehab, and despite the promises he'd made to himself to not interfere with Henry's sessions with Kari, he couldn't stop his feet from taking him to the rehab side of the complex.

Purposely, he'd cleared his afternoon so he could be free while she was in the building—in total opposition to his promise. Abruptly, he was catapulted back to a previous conversation with Raph and Henry.

His partners thought to warn him away from becoming too involved with his *Kichōna's* care, citing conflict of interest. When it came to Kari, Daisuke didn't give a shit about conflict of interest. He didn't *completely* trust anyone when it came to her well-being.

Weeks earlier

"JD, man, come on. You have to see the situation you're putting HJR in. It's clear you want to have more than a doctor patient relationship with Miss Frost. You shouldn't be anywhere near her case,"

Raphael tried to reason with Daisuke. Gathered in Raphael's office, they'd just finished their Monday morning staff meeting.

Shooting a piercing glance in Raphael's direction, Daisuke demanded, "What do you expect me to do? Let that idiot Cotton oversee her treatment? It'll rain gold from heaven before I let him do more than watch from the sidewalk."

Attempting to clarify Raphael's statement, Henry interjected, "JD, we're not saying let Cotton take the case. What we're saying is you have to consider the optics. How does it look for a doctor at HJR to become romantically involved with a patient?"

"We're not romantically involved," Daisuke spat out.

"Yet," Raphael added on.

*"You're not romantically involved **yet**. We all know it's just a matter of time. Once it happens, you'll put all of us in a potentially compromising position."*

"How?" Daisuke questioned.

"How would we be compromised by two consenting adults deciding to spend time together or enter into a relationship?"

"Would she even know she had a choice in the matter?" Raphael challenged.

"What the fuck is that supposed to mean?" Daisuke growled. "Are you saying I would force myself on her?"

At the implication he would harm Kari, his body coiled tightly with tension.

"Come on, man. I'm not saying you'd force her into sex or anything like that, but you basically took over her medical care, and her treatment plan without asking her if it was what she wanted. We don't have a contract with the Fantasy and for all you know, there could have been another doctor she wanted to use besides Cotton—or us for that matter," Raphael continued in his quest to reason with Daisuke.

*Hardening his gaze even more, Daisuke argued, "She deserves the best care possible. **We** are the best care possible. Period."*

"JD, I'm not saying she can't afford us, but what if the Fantasy won't cover the expenses?" Henry asked.

Piling on to Henry's concerns, Raphael couldn't seem to stop himself from adding, "Let's not forget, you grossly overstepped with Cotton. If he decides to, he could cause a stink about being iced out."

"Cotton doesn't scare me. I know too much about him, and he'd do best to stay out of my business. As for cost, I'll take care of it. All of it," Daisuke bit out, ignoring the exasperated expressions on his partners' faces.

"I'm done discussing this. I have patients to see." Having said his piece, he walked out of Raphael's office.

"Dr. Sano?" The office assistant's voice snapped him back into the present.

Daisuke turned to the young man walking toward him. "Yes?"

"There's a call for you on line two." The young man gestured back down the hallway.

Daisuke turned back to the doorway of the rehab area.

"Take a message."

"Sir, I tried. They said it was urgent."

The young man said nervously as he shuffled from one foot to another.

Blowing out a breath of frustration, Daisuke turned back toward his office. Shooting the kid a semi-smile to calm his nervousness, Daisuke swallowed his own disappointment. He didn't even catch a glimpse of Kari. Resolving to finish the call as quickly as possible, he planned to at least speak to her for a few minutes before she left.

Muted steps could be heard thumping against the tiled flooring as he stalked back toward his office to take the call. *And it better damn well be an actual emergency.* The office assistant, a kid barely out of his teens, wisely stepped out of Daisuke's path.

Chapter Four

KARI

The pinging of Kari's phone pierced her bubble of quietness.

"Ugh!"

She groaned in complaint of the chiming noise from the doorbell ringing through her home. Snatching her cellphone from the coffee table, she raised her head from the pillow she was hugging. *Who could possibly be at my door at 10am?*

Just when she'd finally convinced her mother it wasn't necessary to spend all day every day watching over her, people were popping up on her doorstep. Ever since Kari had convinced her to adjust her visitation schedule, her mother only came to take Kari to therapy, because she still wasn't driving.

Double checking the time, she shook her head. Any close friends and family would be working at this time of day. Tapping the icon to open the app, she pulled up the feed from the doorbell camera.

What she saw made her bolt upright on the couch. *Holy Shit!* Daisuke was standing on her doorstep! *What in the entire hell is going on? Since when does he know where I live?*

Giving herself a quick visual inspection, she took note of the loose black gym shorts and the old orange college t-shirt with the stretched-out neck and peeling letters. When she looked at her feet in the fuzzy purple socks, she groaned. The hand she pushed into her hair felt the curls, wild on one side and smushed on the other, because she neglected to put on her head wrap.

Looking around her living room, she was relieved to see that besides the blanket and pillow she was using, the area was neat and free of clutter. Maybe it wasn't such a bad thing her mom still came over a couple of times a week to at least help her keep things clean.

The doorbell chimed again, and she turned her eyes back to the phone in her hand. Daisuke still stood on her doorstep, only now, he was staring directly into the lens of the doorbell cam. She watched as he pulled his phone from his pocket and tapped the screen.

Seconds later, she almost dropped the phone when it buzzed in her hand and the Kool Moe D song, *I Go to Work,* started playing. Loudly. *Damnit!* Shaking fingers moved to quickly silence the noise, but not quickly enough. She had to either answer the phone or the door or both. It wasn't possible he hadn't heard the music. Seeing him lean in closer to the camera confirmed her fear.

Running one hand through his hair, he pushed the long dark tresses from his face, while he positioned himself closer to the camera. Taking the phone away from his ear, he tapped the screen. The buzzing in Kari's hand stopped as he ended the call. His panty melting voice came through clearly over the speaker.

"*Shi no shin*, I know you can see it's me. Open the door."

Straightening to his full six-foot height, he folded his arms across his impressive chest. Bulging biceps flexed under his fitted black t-shirt.

He stepped back far enough to expose his lower half encased in jeans that fit his thick thighs to perfection. The man did ***not*** skip leg day. *Bless him!* Even without him turning around, she knew the jeans cupped his ass perfectly.

Biting her bottom lip, Kari stared at the camera feed. One of these days, she was going to ask him what *Shi no shin* meant. It was a given he was talking to her, but she wondered what the phrase meant. Her one certainty was that the term was of Japanese origin. Whether it was a term of endearment or an innocuous nickname, she couldn't be sure.

During their daily conversations over the past six weeks, she'd learned a great deal about him. In one of their previous chats, they'd discussed him being first generation Japanese-American. His parents met in the US as college students and decided to stay in America instead of returning home to Japan after graduation.

Trying to help he and his siblings fit in with other American children, his parents gave each of them an American first name and a Japanese middle name. It was while he was in medical school that he decided he preferred his Japanese name and stopped using Johnathan altogether. He told her that parents had always called him Daisuke at home, so the only adjustment was in dealing with those outside of his family unit.

Having grown up bi-lingual, he would randomly sprinkle Japanese words or phrases into their discussions. Most of the time, he would voluntarily translate to English. Most of the time. The exception was when he called her *Shi no shin* or *Kichōna*.

During their talks, when he used those terms, he never explained. He peppered them into their dialogue without offering any explanations. Each time he used one of the pet names, her insides tingled.

Despite their daily conversations, she hadn't had much face-to-face interaction with him. Dr. Williams managed her therapy and Daisuke would drop by at the end to say hello and see how things were progressing. Some days were better than others, but he remained supportive. Supportive, but not the showing up on her threshold kind of supportive.

Slowly, she stood from the sofa. She no longer needed crutches, but she moved slower than usual. She and Dr. Williams were still working on range of motion and flexibility, so she took extra care when moving around. Running the fingers of her free hand through her flattened curls, she tried to hastily fluff them out in an attempt to even out her lopsided bed-head hair style.

Disarming the alarm, she opened the door to Daisuke standing at her entrance looking like a badass from an action movie. Images of one of those movies with hot Asian men fighting, using martial arts, and tossing people through plate-glass windows flit unbidden through her mind's eye. With his arms folded across his chest, he could definitely pass for a super bad boss from the movies.

He looks pissed. But, who does he think he is looking at me like that? Like I've been bad and he was here to dish out my punishment. Kari's initial reaction was to guiltily avert her eyes, but she squashed the inclination to show any type of guilt.

First of all, she had no reason to feel guilt. Secondly, even if she did feel remorse, why would he be the person to invoke such a response? Last time she checked, he had no authority over her. Maybe they were about to find out just how much she was willing to let him get away with.

Drawing her eyebrows together, she questioned his presence "Daisuke, is something wrong? What are you doing here?"

"My queen, people normally greet guests at their door with the word *hello*. Then, they ask them to come in."

Her head rocked back on her shoulders. *Aw hell naw! No he did **not** just try to chastise me! Having people remind me of my manners is starting to grate on my nerves.* Tipping her head to the side, she lifted one eyebrow.

"Excuse you?"

Standing in the doorway, she kept one hand on the doorknob and the other on the doorframe.

Holding up both hands in mock surrender, Daisuke ducked his head.

"Let's start over. Good morning, my queen. If you would kindly step aside, I'll come in and we can talk about why I'm here."

It wasn't quite the about-face Kari was looking for, but she let it slide. Something told her, this was as much of a concession as he would be willing to make. *I'm not always going to let him have his way.*

That's what she told herself as she dropped her arm from the doorframe and stepped back waving him into the foyer. Pushing the door closed, she turned to walk back into the living room.

"—Oopmh!"

The air whooshed from her lungs as she collided with Daisuke's solid body. Strong arms grasped her around her torso, pulling her into a warm, firm chest. She must have turned faster than she realized, because she needed his powerful arms to help maintain her balance.

"Careful, *Kichōna*! We wouldn't want you to re-injure yourself."

Unwrapping one arm, he cradled the side of her face in his large palm, tipping her head back.

Being held so closely to him, Kari's heart hammered in her chest. Other than when he carried her from the basketball court, they had never been so close. Even when he'd come by to chat after her therapy sessions, he didn't get nearly so close. This closeness was different from their short trip to the locker room. Their bodies were pressed together from chest to knee.

With her being only three inches shorter, their hips were almost in perfect alignment. Enough of an alignment for her to feel *him* and his thick bulge pressed into her lower abdomen.

Why in the world am I focusing on his lower anatomy? Because a bulge like that is hard to miss. That's why. Butterflies erupted in her stomach and her breathing quickened.

Daisuke's intense gaze captured her eyes.

"How are you feeling this morning? Henry told me you rescheduled your therapy for today and tomorrow. He also said you weren't feeling well at the end of yesterday's session. What is going on to cause you to cancel physical therapy? We've discussed this, you have to be consistent to see results."

Momentarily distracted from the bulging appendage pressing into her middle, Kari crinkled her brow, peering into his eyes.

"Let me get this right. You came over here because I rescheduled a couple of appointments?"

"Yes, you canceled, **and** you didn't answer when I called last night or this morning. I was concerned."

Holding her securely to his body, he continued to cup her face—his thumb stroking her cheek.

"How did you know my address?"

Suddenly mute, Daisuke didn't respond to her question. Giving her a pointed look with a single raised eyebrow, he offered her no words. The urge to melt into his embrace and absorb his warmth rode her, but she fought it off.

Somewhere within herself, she found some resolve. She had questions, and she was determined to get answers. *Why is he behaving as though they are more than passing acquaintances or even new friends?*

Even as she had the thought, she knew she was trying to fool herself again. *Ok fine. They were more than passing acquaintances but they were far from the kind of intimacy she saw in his eyes.*

The way he was holding her was not even close to being platonic. As good as it felt, she wanted some clarity before falling any farther down the proverbial rabbit hole.

If anyone asked, she would blame her sudden bravery on hormones. Her menstrual cramps were being especially brutal this month. It was always worse for her when she didn't keep her regular, strenuous, exercise routine. The accompanying hormonal shifts were no walk in the park either.

The relentless pain and her snarky attitude were part of the reason she rescheduled her sessions. Besides her less-than-stellar attitude, she had an appearance commitment scheduled for the following day.

Having her question being answered with silence and the raised eyebrow increased her irritation.

"Don't look at me like that," she snipped.

"Look at you like what?" He responded smoothly, as if he gave zero fucks about her rising annoyance.

"Like I should already know the answer to my question. I don't. I don't know how you know where I live. I don't even know how you knew my phone number to call me. Don't get me wrong, I wondered those things when the flowers were delivered and you started calling. But, now, you're showing up at my house and I need answers. You do know the fact that you have such information, without me supplying it, is bordering on stalker-ish behavior, right?"

Pressing her hands to his ridiculously hard chest, she pushed to place some distance between them. Thankfully, for her piece of mind, he allowed some space between them; but he didn't release her completely. The warmth from his hands on her and the heat radiating off his body were still wreaking havoc on her resolve to get answers.

"*Kichōna*, how long have you known me?" Piercing eyes held her captive.

"A little more than a year, but what does the length of time I've known you have to do with anything?"

Kari was far from dense, but she wasn't following his line of questioning. It's possible his question was a tactic to avoid directly responding to the stalker comment. Squeezing her biceps, he held her gaze.

"Everything. In all the time we've known each other, did you ever take me as a man who isn't resourceful?"

"Again, what does that have to do with my question?"

Internally, she patted herself on the back for staying on the subject and not letting the reality of being scant inches away from his big body turn her brain to mush.

"As a resourceful man, I make it my business to know information I deem important."

His eyes swept the length of her body, making his unspoken point abundantly clear. She was included in the scope of things he considered important.

"Daisuke..." she returned in an exasperated sigh.

"Fine... I took the information from the documents you filled out. Now can we sit? Has your curiosity been satisfied?"

Waving his arm, he pointed to the opening separating the foyer from the den. It was unsettling to know he'd gotten her info from her paperwork, rather than asking her for it, and she wasn't sure how she felt about it. If he'd asked, she would have given it to him, even if she had been operating under the illusion he wasn't interested in her the same way she was interested in him.

Maybe her teammates were right, Daisuke had bypassed friendship and sailed into another arena entirely. Showing up on her doorstep because of missed appointments and phone calls, said he was far more invested than any of them realized.

DAISUKE

Daisuke was beyond caring about the boundaries he was pushing by showing up at Kari's home. Cutting her previous session short, cancelling her next two, and going radio silent on him was a no-go. A successful recovery from her injury was very important to her, so for her to miss therapy, he knew something had to be seriously wrong, and he had every intention of getting to the bottom of it.

Moving back to the sofa, she sat near a pillow and blanket she must have been using before he arrived. Watching her movements, he looked for a sign or some clue to help him figure out what illness caused her to bail. Was it depression that drove her to hole up in her home, apparently napping? It was a possibility if she thought she wasn't progressing as quickly as she'd hoped.

Athletes who are used to performing at a high level can be susceptible to depression after an injury forces them to slow down. Giving himself a mental shake, he dismissed the idea. It didn't align with what he saw in the weeks of therapy with his *Kichōna*.

After they settled on the couch, he brought the topic back to what he wanted to know. Stretching his arm across the short distance separating them, he touched the back of his hand to her forehead and under her chin. There was no lingering; he held his fingers in place long enough to get a good gauge of her body temperature.

"*Kichōna*, tell me what's going on. Are you ill? You don't feel feverish."

Turning her face forward, she averted her eyes. "Do you do this for all of your patients?"

Lightly grasping her chin in his hand, he turned her face back towards his.

"We both know you aren't just a patient. We are much too far gone to pretend, *Shi no shin*."

Caressing her cheek, he drifted toward her plush lips—marveling at the softness of her skin. He scrutinized every detail, so he didn't miss the grimace flitting across her visage.

"Don't hide from me. I can feel your tension. Tell me what's going on. I may be able to help."

His voice was softer but laced with steel—conveying his determination.

Kari sighed, "I'm not feeling well. Can we just leave it at that?"

"No. We can't. Not feeling well, isn't a reason to cancel and reschedule. You've come to therapy with soreness, aches and various other pains. What makes this different?"

She flicked her eyes away, but not before he saw the fire flash within their depths. Then, seeming to come to a decision, she spoke again.

"Daisuke, can we not do this? My issue is personal and I'd really rather not discuss it."

Realization plucked Daisuke in his forehead as soundly as his mother had thumped him during his rambunctious childhood. Releasing her chin, he sat back on the sofa.

"I've made you uncomfortable," he gave a resigned exhale. "My apologies. In my concern I pushed too hard."

Waiting a few silent moments, he tried to think of a way to eliminate the discomfort between them. He hadn't intended to put her on the spot and make her uncomfortable. Daisuke needed to try a different tactic, because his current method wasn't working the way he'd hoped.

Just when he started to despair, an idea presented itself to him. "Do you like hot tea?"

Scrunching her brow, she swung her eyes back to his.

"I do…"

It was obvious she didn't know where he was going with his question, but he continued.

"Do you prefer loose tea leaves or bags?"

Her face still a mask of confusion, Kari replied.

"I usually get bags. I don't have an infuser to use loose leaves."

With a quick nod of acknowledgement, Daisuke stood from the couch. Giving her no time to ask what he was doing, he just walked into her kitchen and took a quick inventory.

Opening her refrigerator and looking through her cabinets, he noted she didn't have what he needed to implement his plan. He was sure she could hear the banging and muffled sounds of him rummaging, but she didn't follow him into the kitchen, nor did she call out to him. Done with his search, he walked back into the den.

"Find what you're looking for?" she asked, her voice dripping with sarcasm.

"I did thanks," he ignored her tone. Pulling his keys from his pocket, he pinned her with a stern look.

"I need to step out for a bit. I'll be back in thirty minutes." Daisuke didn't wait for a response; he simply turned on his heel and walked out.

Chapter Five

KARI

True to his word, thirty minutes later Daisuke was back at her door. This time, he was carrying reusable shopping bags in both hands. The bags were bulging with what, Kari couldn't tell. Spying what appeared to be kale poking from the top of one of the bags, her face screwed up in distaste. *Who does he think is going to eat that?*

"What's all this?"

She asked, trailing him into her kitchen. Feeling some kind of way about him marching himself into her house taking over, she watched him speculatively. Appearing completely comfortable, he breezed by her as though it was an everyday occurrence for him to be in her kitchen. The purposeful, confident way he moved about in her space almost convinced her to let his lack of response slide. Almost.

Continuing to maneuver about her kitchen, he unpacked the shopping bags. In a very short amount of time, he looked as if he'd learned her storage system—judging from the way he was pulling various dishes, utensils and small appliances out onto the countertop.

"You wanna let me in on what you're doing? You know, since this is my house and all."

The hint of sarcasm in her words seemed to float past him. Giving a negligent roll of his shoulders, he lifted his eyes away from his task to capture hers.

"Patience. You'll see."

The deep timbre of his voice carried his statement over as a command, demanding her compliance.

Huffing, Kari didn't utter another word. At least not out loud. Silently, she was giving him the business.

Silently.

This side of Daisuke was new to her, so maybe a watch and see course of action was the best option. All would be revealed soon enough. Plopping herself onto a barstool at the counter separating her small breakfast area from her kitchen, she propped her chin on her hand, watching him.

In short order, Daisuke set a mug of hot water in front of her. Ripping open a tea packet, he placed the bag in the water.

"Let this steep for five minutes, then drink it," He instructed, placing a honey bear and spoon next to the steaming mug.

Lifting the tag, she read the inspirational message written on it. *'Traveling the road alone, you can reach your destination. Traveling with a friend can turn the journey into an adventure.'*

Hmph. Cute and poignant. The cuteness didn't quell her desire for answers, though.

"Okay, Mr. Bossy Pants. What kind of tea is this and why should I drink it?"

Quirking an eyebrow, he lifted his head from the cutting board he'd just placed on the countertop. "It's a blend of tea leaves designed to relieve the symptoms you're experiencing."

What exactly did he think he knew about my symptoms?

"What do you mean the symptoms I'm experiencing? I never said what was going on, other than I don't feel well."

Showing up uninvited, while she felt like a grungy sack of pooh was embarrassing enough. Him acknowledging the elephant in the room made her want to crawl through the floor. Heat crept up her face just thinking of him knowing exactly why she begged off therapy. This whole thing was a level of intimacy it could take couples years to achieve —and they weren't even a couple.

Pausing from chopping the freshly washed kale, he covered her hand with his.

"There's no reason to be embarrassed. It's a natural process; it's just harder for some than others."

Giving her hand a squeeze, he reassured her, "This doesn't have to be a big deal, *Kichōna*. Drink your tea."

"Why are you acting like this is normal?"

She was genuinely baffled. Who wants to discuss their period with their super-hot crush? No one. That's who.

"Because it *is* normal. Until you experience pregnancy or menopause, you'll continue to have a period."

He started back chopping kale like he wasn't discussing a subject he should be pretending didn't exist. At least if she had her way, he would *not* be standing his sexy ass in her kitchen chatting about her menstrual cycle.

"This totally is not a conversation I want to have with you, or anyone, for that matter. Boundaries, man..."

Adding honey to the tea and stirring it allowed Kari to avoid his far too observant gaze.

"Why do we need to avoid talking about something so natural? I won't pretend to know precisely how you feel, but I want to help make it better."

When he looked at her, his eyes burned with intensity. "For me, there is no boundary when you're in pain and I can do something about it."

That shut her up. Any other day, with anyone else, this wouldn't be the end of it, but there was no arguing with his logic. If it wasn't clear to her before, it was then.

When he told her that it was his job to take care of her, he meant that shit. *Well, damn.* Properly chastised, she added honey to her tea, stirred it briefly and took a sip from the mug. *If you can't beat 'em, join 'em.*

～

DAISUKE

Daisuke knew he was being overbearing, but Kari was so stubborn. If he didn't push, she'd never let him in. With a little intensive **coaxing**, he convinced her to drink the smoothie he'd made. To convince her to try it, he had to drink some first, and promise her that she wouldn't be able to taste the kale.

He'd chosen the fruits and vegetables specifically to relieve her cramps and bloating—something he'd learned partially from his mother and two younger sisters as well as natural healing classes in med school.

After her smoothie, he settled her back on the sofa with the light-weight, super flexible heating pad he'd bought on his outing. Surprisingly, she didn't give him any push back and they settled in for an afternoon of binge-watching *Wu Assassins* on *Netflix*.

Keeping up intermittent banter while they watched, each gave their theories on who they thought were the good guys and bad guys. Only the *mildest* tinge of jealousy snaked through his chest when she gushed over Byron Mann's character, Uncle Six. Daisuke may have been proud of himself for not taking the bait, but he made a mental note to avoid introducing her to his friend Jian anytime soon. His med-school friend bore an uncanny resemblance to the actor.

Four episodes later, he reluctantly called an end to the marathon. Duty called, and he needed to get back to the office to see a patient. The four hours they'd spent together weren't nearly enough. As much as he'd rather stay with Kari, it wasn't in the cards today. Closing the small gap between them, he ran a finger along the exposed skin from her elbow to the back of her hand.

"So, should I tell Henry you'll be able to make your appointment tomorrow afternoon after all? Do you think you'll be up to it?" He asked, enjoying the feel of her skin beneath his fingers.

"Um... No. I do feel better, but I rescheduled tomorrow's appointment because I have to make an appearance at an event that I booked in the spring. I'd forgotten about it until my publicist called to go over my calendar for the month."

Tangling his fingers with hers, he waited for her to tell him more about what she'd be doing. Realizing she had no intention of elaborating, he asked.

"What kind of event is it?"

Thankfully, she didn't balk at him pressing for more information. She simply responded to his question.

"It's a back-to-school event at the Logan City Public Library. I'm a featured reader. It's a part of my campaign promoting literacy. Even if I didn't want to do it, I wouldn't feel right canceling on them so close to the event date. They've put a lot of effort into advertising to try to get as many parents as possible to bring their kids out for the occasion."

Nodding to show he understood, he squeezed her fingers. "What time does it start?"

He felt her stiffen ever so slightly before answering. Confused eyes met his own and a little line creased her otherwise smooth forehead.

"It starts at three o'clock. Why?"

"I'm not going into the office tomorrow, so I'll take you. I can pick you up at noon, we can grab a quick lunch and go over to the library afterwards."

It wasn't an offer. Basically, he was telling her what was going to happen. Except, the look on her face said she wasn't on board with his high-handed methods. *Too bad.* He'd grown used to seeing or talking to her daily. He wasn't about to let her deprive him of his fix. Not if he could help it.

Shaking her head, she tried to decline the mandate he hadn't bothered to disguise as an offer.

"You don't have to spend your day off driving me around. One of my teammates is going to come and get me, since she has to be there anyway."

Tipping his head to the side, he regarded her with curiosity.

"Is there a reason you don't want me to take you?"

In Daisuke's mind, his suggestion was perfectly reasonable. He'd take her where she needed to go and they would have an opportunity to spend more one-on-one time together. *Win—Win.*

Attempting to remove her fingers from their entanglement with his, Kari released an exasperated huff.

"Daisuke, what's really going on here? I'm not just talking about today. Ever since I was injured, you've been acting differently towards me. We've always been friendly, but lately you've been... intense. Intense and demanding. You bullied poor Dr. Cotton into stepping aside and I swear it seems like you told everyone at the practice not to let me leave unless you were with me."

Gripping her fingers, holding on, not allowing her to pull away, he contemplated which words to use to convey how he felt—without coming off like a lunatic stalker.

"*Shi no shin*, I've never told you about the legend of my ancestors, have I?"

Confusion and irritation were painted across her brow; Kari shook her head.

"I didn't believe I had. My family name, Sano means '*small field*', but there are some with the name who are descendants of the samurai warrior class. My family is among that group."

Untangling their fingers, he began to trace patterns on her palm while he spoke.

"Most people only know of the fierce warrior persona of the samurai, but they don't know the reason for that fierceness. The key expectations of all samurai were for them to maintain justice, courage, benevolence, respect, honesty, honor, and loyalty. They were so fearless in battle because they were fighting to protect their families and elders to whom they were loyal."

Using his penetrating stare to keep her focused on him, he continued.

"During the time that we've known each other, we have grown into what *you* may consider a friendship. *For me*, you are my family. It goes against everything that I am for me to be able to protect and provide for you in your time of need, yet not do so."

He shook his head, "I refuse."

Knowing he probably overwhelmed her with his admission, he added nothing further to his statement. He made no mention of how he knew she was meant to be his, or how his heart thumped in his chest at the very thought of her. *His Queen.*

Raising her hand to his lips, he placed a kiss on her palm.

"I will see you tomorrow at noon."

With a quick pat and squeeze to her hand, he scooped his keys from the coffee table and stood to leave.

"I'll lock the door on my way out. Use the app on your phone to set the alarm."

With concerted effort, he ignored the daggers she was shooting in his direction. While her happiness would always be his priority, he was putting her on notice regarding who she was to him and who he was to her. She was his *Kichōna*, his *Shi no shin*—his *Precious*, his *Heart*. Standing on the sidelines of her life was no longer a possibility.

Chapter Six

KARI

As soon as the door closed behind Daisuke, Kari grabbed her phone. Not to follow his instructions and set the alarm, but to call her most trusted confidant—her cousin Candy. Candy was far more than a cousin. As the saying goes, *cousins are our first friends*. At least for Kari it was true. Being an only child, she didn't have siblings to turn to with her secrets or to get in trouble with, but she had Candy.

She'd always had Candy. Squished between two sisters with large demanding personalities, Candy was in many ways the typical middle child. Always the one trying to keep the peace, she'd grown into someone who always seemed to be ready with level-headed advice when Kari needed it. Not that she needed it often, but she absolutely needed it now.

Her fingers danced across her thigh nervously tapping as she waited for Candy to answer the phone. She wasn't sure if her cousin was on a set or had a private booking. She hoped against hope that whatever the schedule, Candy would see her name on the display and answer the call. Relief flooded her body when the ringing stopped, and Candy's husky alto reached her ears.

"Hello?"

"Candy!"

"What?"

"You will never guess what just happened!"

Kari's voice trembled in nervous excitement. She felt like a teenager again instead of a grown, thirty-two-year-old, woman. It had been forever since she had butterflies in her stomach or anticipated being with a man the way she was with Daisuke.

"Don't keep me waiting chick! I only have about fifteen minutes before I have to head back to this trailer to start working on Miss Thang's face for this evening shoot."

Kari could always tell if Candy liked the person she was working with by the nickname she gave them. If she liked them, they were all the sweet complimentary names in the book. If she didn't particularly care for them or they were difficult, she usually called them, Miss Thang or Mister Man. Whoever this client was, Kari knew from the nickname that Candy didn't care much for working with her.

As a sought-after Make-up Artist, Candy worked with a ton of high-profile people. So, she rarely gave out names unless she had an agreement with the actress or model. Even then, she liked to play it close to the vest. Not talking about her A-list clientele allowed many people to underestimate her talent.

But, that was a story for another day. Pulling herself together, Kari launched into a verbal tsunami full of run on sentences and very few breaths. She'd placed the call on speaker, so her hands flapped about as she spoke and she shifted in her seat unable to sit still.

"Hey, hey, hey, Queenie! Slow down. Take a breath. I know I said I was short on time, but you don't have to speed talk your way through what sounded like might be some good tea if you give me a chance to sip it."

Taking a deep breath in; Kari held it a moment then let it out slowly. After a few inhales and exhales she sat up straighter on the sofa and tried again.

"Ok. Ok. Ok."

"Are you in control now?"

"I think so."

"Alright. Start from the beginning."

"Ok. So, you know how I told you that my cramps have been kicking my ass since I can't work out like I normally do?"

"Uh-huh."

"Well, I'm lying on the couch this morning, and my doorbell rings. Who's at my door you ask?"

"I didn't but I know you'll tell me. So, continue."

"It's Daisuke. As in Dr. J. Daisuke Sano. As in the hot ass man that you kept telling me was into me for the past year and I kept saying he wasn't. Because... Look at him! You've seen him. I don't have to tell you."

"Yes, I've seen him and yes he's hella fine. But, have you seen *you*? Why wouldn't he want you? You don't need me to tell you how much women pay me so I can make them look even half as good as you do with a little eyeliner and a light gloss on your lips. Don't start with me. Now, get back to the tea."

"Right. So, I'm looking a hot mess, because... hello Auntie's kicking my ass. I don't have time to do anything about it, so I get myself together mentally and let him inside."

Kari heard some shuffling in the background and Candy's breathing picked up. Figuring she was on borrowed time while Candy walked back to the trailer, she pushed on. She didn't go into a complete play-by-play of the past four hours but gave her the highlights.

While Kari still thought it was somewhat embarrassing to discuss her menstrual symptoms with Daisuke, Candy thought it was super cute and romantic that he wanted to take care of her that way. Candy practically gushed at everything Kari told her they did over those four hours and completely glossed over him showing up unannounced to begin with.

After letting her in on how Daisuke had insinuated himself into the events lined up for the next day, Kari asked the question that was really burning her brain from the moment she placed the call.

"I totally misread this whole thing, didn't I?"

"Yep."

"You didn't have to answer so quick."

"Why play around? I've been telling you for the longest that your interest in him wasn't one sided."

"I know..."

"Do you? Do you really? Because, I seem to recall one of the few times I was actually free to come to a game, I told you afterwards that the man eats you up with his eyes. It's like you're the only person who matters. The only time he acknowledges anyone else for more than a second, it's because they have somehow entered your orbit."

"It's not that intense."

"It really is."

"What am I supposed to do now?"

"What do you want to do?"

"Don't do that! I called you for advice."

Kari's face scrunched into an epic pout even though she knew Candy couldn't see her. So, the facial expression was completely ineffective in swaying her friend.

"No ma'am. I'm not telling you what to do. You're going to have to put on your big girl panties and decide for yourself how you want to move forward with your sexy doctor."

Kari gazed at nothing while pulling up the image of Daisuke standing on her porch looking scrumptious in his all-black ensemble that hugged his frame perfectly. The memory brought a crooked grin to her face.

"He is sexy ain't he?"

"You ain't never lied."

Silence reigned on the line for a few moments while Kari contemplated her situation and if she was ready for what it seemed Daisuke was putting on the table. Candy didn't rush her, even though she could hear people calling out to her friend as they held their silence.

"I'm gonna do it."

"That's good... What are you going to do?"

"I'm going to let him take me to lunch tomorrow and to the event that I have at the library."

"Queenie, I hate to break it to you babe, but I don't think that part is optional. What's optional is if you actually allow him into your life as more than just a friendly acquaintance."

"Yeah..."

"So, give it to me on the real. Stop tip-toeing around it."

"After I got over my initial shock of him being here today, I had a really good time talking to him and just... being... You know?"

Kari's fingers toyed with the edge of the blanket draped over her lap as she exposed her feelings. Candy was one of the few people she could be vulnerable with, but doing so still made her slightly uneasy.

"I get it. So, what are you going to do about it?"

"I'm going to give it a chance."

"And have the talk?"

"The talk?"

"Don't play. The talk. Don't make assumptions. Get it out in the open. Y'all are both too grown to play around. How old is he anyway?"

"Ummm... Thirty-seven?"

"Are you asking me or telling me?"

"I'm trying to remember... No. He's thirty-eight. He had a birthday recently."

"Like I said. Y'all are both too grown to play around. Go on your date tomorrow. Have fun, but at some point, get some clarity on what the two of you are doing. Is the date the start of something or just a friendly outing?"

"I know you're right, but you just gave me even more to think about and it's making me nervous all over again."

"I know it does no good to tell you not to be nervous; so how about I come over tomorrow morning and give you a facial and make up your face in that ultra-natural look that you like?"

"Would you?"

"You know I gotchu. I gotta go. Miss Thang is here."

DAISUKE

As he maneuvered his vehicle into the left side of Kari's driveway, Daisuke took note of the sleek black luxury SUV parked on the opposite side. *Who the hell is that?* His brow creased in a hard frown at the thought that she may have contacted someone else to take her to the day's events despite what they'd discussed the previous day.

They had a plan. Or at least *he* had a plan. She seemed to be on board when he left yesterday. She hadn't said anything about changing her mind when he texted her to let her know he was on his way to pick her up this morning. Ending his mental speculation, he shut off the engine and stepped out of his truck. Only one way to find out what was going on, and that was to go inside—or at least ring the bell.

When he reached the end of the walk nearest the front door, it swung open and out walked a smiling, laughing duo comprised of his *Kichōna* and a woman who looked vaguely familiar. She was roughly the same height as Kari with similar features, but not identical. The second woman was quite lovely and had he any interest in anyone outside of his *Shi no shin,* her deep brown skin and statuesque figure would definitely have his attention.

As it stood, he only appreciated her beauty in the sense of internally acknowledging it and nothing more. No matter how attractive, this woman wasn't the one who made his heart leap. Only Kari did that.

Turning from one another, they noticed his silent presence on the walkway. Smiles still intact, they both offered greetings. Gesturing between him and the woman, Kari proceeded to make introductions.

"Candace Hampton, this is Daisuke Sano. Daisuke, meet my cousin and bestie, Candace."

With a radiant smile that reached her dark sparkling eyes, Candace reached out to shake his hand, "It's nice to meet you formally, Dr. Sano. I've seen you at the games, but never had a chance to say hello."

"Please, call me Daisuke. I thought I recognized your face, but I couldn't quite place you. It's nice to meet you as well."

"If I'm going to call you Daisuke, you have to call me Candy."

"Deal."

Smiling politely at Candy, Daisuke nodded and turned his eyes to Kari. He always found her stunning, but she seemed to glow even more than usual. Her russet brown skin shone with what appeared to be golden undertones. Her normally massive curls were swept into a high ponytail arranged at the crown of her head with the spring coils looking like a semi-tamed curly afro.

He was no expert at women's hairstyles and his experience with black women's hair was minimal, so he was sure his view of the style was more simplistic that whatever effort she took to make it look that way. Hungry eyes roved over her form taking in the champagne-colored romper lightly hugging her figure and stopping midway down her creamy thighs leaving a large expanse of her supple legs on display.

As he made it to the flat, strappy sandals on her feet, a clearing throat had him snapping his eyes back up. A flush crept up his neck at the realization that his perusal hadn't been quick nor had it gone unnoticed. His embarrassment wasn't in his action, it was in the fact that he hadn't been as smooth about it as he thought.

"Well... I think that's my cue to leave. You two kids have fun! I have... something... somewhere that's not here. Later!"

Hitching a tote bag onto one shoulder, Candy gave Kari a quick hug, nodded to Daisuke and strode down the walkway to her SUV. Taking advantage of the moment, he took the few short steps necessary to bring him right next to Kari on the porch.

"Are you ready, or do you need a few more minutes?" He asked as he drank her in with his eyes. The simple outfit was elevated by her athletically curvy body. Bright eyes met his own and the corners of her lips lifted in a smile.

"No. I'm ready. Just let me grab my bag and keys."

"Ok. I'll wait here."

While Kari went back inside, he watched as Candy navigated her way from the driveway onto the street. By the time his *Kichōna* returned with her things, her cousin was out of sight having turned the corner to the road leaving the subdivision.

The drive to the restaurant was filled with light, basic conversation. He delved a little more into the nature of the back-to-school event and she told him the reasons she was so passionate about reading and providing books to children—especially children of color.

He hadn't actually thought of the way she explained it, but he could see the merits. Opening a young person's mind with entertaining books also opened then to knowledge and the possibilities of being more than what they saw on TV or social media. He made a mental note to see how he could become more involved with a similar initiative. He already participated in events to help Asian Americans connect with their cultures, but he saw opportunities in branching out.

There was a lull in the conversation as they ate, and he could feel a bit of tension creep into Kari's posture. Mentally, he thought back over the conversation to try to pinpoint what or when something happened, but he came up empty. Everything seemed to be going fine. She was relaxed, smiling and talking about her passion away from the basketball court. Unable to stand her discomfort, he broke the silence.

"Is everything ok, *Shi no shin*?"

"Hm? Oh. Yes. Everything's fine."

"Are you sure?"

"Of course. Why do you ask?"

"You seem a little tense."

Daisuke's eyes tracked her movements as she lowered the fork poised over her plate and shifted in her seat. As much as he wanted to, he didn't rush her to speak. He waited quietly as she looked everywhere but at him. Eventually, she returned her gaze to his face, and he could see she'd come to a decision.

"What are we doing?"

"Having lunch..."

"No. Please don't do that. Please don't pretend you don't know what I'm asking. This is awkward enough as it is."

"Ok... I apologize. I wasn't trying to be flip with you. I just wasn't immediately on the same page."

"Are we on the same page now?"

"I think so. You want to know my intentions with you."

"Yes."

"What do you think?"

"I don't know. That's why I'm asking. I don't want to assume something that isn't there. Over the past year, we've had conversations here and there and we've gotten to know each other more since my injury. That's been great."

"But...?"

"No but. I'm just trying to figure out if this is us building a friendship or is this something else?"

After asking her question, her eyes glued themselves to the remaining contents of the plate in front of her. He was so focused on her and her words, he couldn't even recall what was on the plate she was staring at so intensely.

"*Kichōna*, look at me."

The seconds ticked by so slowly, time almost seemed to stand still as he waited for her to comply and return her focus to him instead of her mostly eaten lunch. After what seemed like an eternity, but was probably only a few seconds, she lifted her head.

"I am your friend. I want to do things with you that friends do together."

"Ok..."

"I'm not done."

"Oh."

"I also want to build a relationship with you. I want the chance to get to know you the way a man gets to know a woman he wants in his life as more than a platonic friend."

Silence stretched between them again following his revelation. Picking up his drink, he downed the contents trying to wet his throat. It had gone dry at the thought that she didn't feel even remotely close to what he felt for her. Wondering if he'd read too much into her responses to him, he waited once again for her to process his words.

"So, just so we're clear. This is a date?"

"Yes, my queen. This is definitely a date."

"And after this?"

"Another date, maybe more phone calls and we'll go from there. How does that sound to you?"

"That sounds like a start."

Her plump lips spread in a sweet but sly smile which finally allowed him to relax. She wasn't trying to end things with him. She needed reassurance the same as he did.

Returning her smile with one of his own, he gave in to the urge to touch her. Clasping her hand where it rested on the table, he brought it to his lips and kissed the back of it softly.

"We all have to start somewhere. We'll start here."

"Ok."

"Ok."

Watching all of the tension release from her body turned out to be what he needed to fully enjoy the rest of the meal. Before long, they were done. He paid the bill, helped her from her seat and escorted her from the table with his hand pressed against her lower back.

Heads turned as they moved through the restaurant, and it took him a moment to consider that the stares could be because they made such a striking couple. Or, it could be fans surprised to see one of their favorite athletes out in public. It's possible it was a combination of both.

He couldn't blame them for staring. His woman was beautiful. He was a very lucky man. Daisuke's face, to anyone watching looked rather stoic. In reality, he was practically giddy to be out with Kari openly. He was even looking forward to a library full of children to cap off the day.

Chapter Seven

KARI

"Again!" The basketball came flying back to her. She caught it before it could make contact with her body. Dr. Williams...No... Henry. He'd insisted she call him Henry. Henry stood between her and the goal on the indoor basketball court. Dressed similarly to her, in a loose t-shirt and basketball shorts, he was putting her through her paces.

Sweat rolled down Kari's face and dripped from her chin. Swiping a sweatband covered wrist across her forehead, she tried to keep the salty perspiration out of her eyes. Today's rehab session focused on improving her mobility by requiring her to execute movements she'd perform during a game. Internally, she cursed Henry's knowledge of how an athlete's body moved when playing a particular sport.

The drills he designed were thorough, pushing her as close to her limit as they dared. She was still hesitant to make quick stops and shoot jumpers. Phantom knee pains kept her from fully committing. She slowed to a stop instead of the quick stops she was known for, and her trademark jumper was unrecognizable—with her only managing to elevate a few inches off the floor instead of the several inches she'd always been able to achieve. Knowing she wasn't giving it one hundred percent would normally cause her to dig deeper and commit herself to the task until she met and exceeded her goal.

That was before. Before she'd experienced a knee to knee collision resulting in her writhing on the floor in pain. Before months of recovery —of which she was just barely more than halfway complete. *You've got to get your head on straight. You can do this!* Encouragement from her inner cheerleader wasn't quite doing the job, as she contemplated her next move.

Dribbling the ball, she cut left, zipping past him and laying the ball into the net. Retrieving the ball after the lay-up, she dribbled back to the top of the key. Try as she might, she couldn't ignore the disappointed look on his face. She'd purposely cut left instead of right, away from her injured knee. Not coming close to pushing herself enough.

"Do it again!" Daisuke's voice boomed into the space startling both Kari and Henry. "This time you **will** go to your right. Only, you won't face Henry, you'll try to get past me."

"JD –" Henry objected before Daisuke cut him off.

"No, Henry. She isn't pushing herself and she knows it." Piercing her with sharp eyes, his expression left no room for argument.

"Again!"

He demanded, replacing Henry's shorter, bulkier frame with his own. Dressed in scrubs and running shoes, he was in no way outfitted to play basketball, but he appeared to give zero fucks about his lack of proper clothing. His only compromise was to whip his hair into a low man-bun before lifting his arms and bending his knees—getting into a defensive stance in front of her.

I'm getting sick of him thinking he can boss me around! He doesn't know what I'm feeling. He isn't in my skin. Narrowing her eyes at him, she tried to shake off the voice in her head contradicting her even as she had her complaining thoughts.

He **did** have an idea of what she was feeling, because they'd discussed it at length. He could also tell she wasn't driving herself the way she should. The two had spent a considerable amount of time together over the past month. Adding that time to the previous year, he knew her far better than Henry. Grimacing, she grudgingly acknowledged the truth of his words—internally. She wouldn't admit it out loud.

Since the day he showed up on her doorstep, things had taken a turn in their relationship. Trying to live in the moment, she didn't question it. She just enjoyed the attention and getting to know him better.

He surprised her with his level of involvement at the back-to-school event. One of the readers wasn't able to make it, so Daisuke stepped in to read Grace Byers' *I Am Enough* to an eager group of elementary school kids. Glowing, excited faces, with huge smiles, filled his audience of primarily African American girls. Apparently, human females of all ages were drawn to his handsome face and powerful aura.

In the weeks after that first lunch, they'd had *Netflix* binge-a-thons, and a few dinners out. He designated himself as her chauffeur, until she started driving again. Shamelessly, he invited himself to her family's Labor Day cookout.

Wonder of wonders, he managed to survive nosey Aunt Bonita and even Kari's catty cousin Cassandra. Candy, who was supposed to be on Kari's side, fed into Aunt Bonita's intrusive speculation by giving them her cute-couple thumbs up and said she'd happily serve as godmother to the adorable little Blasian babies in their future.

She also suggested Kari talk to McKenna about a possible double wedding with her and her new beau Driscoll. Seeing as McKenna and Driscoll were just as engaged as Kari and Daisuke, the suggestion was severely premature. *Some best friend I have.*

Daisuke and Kari even attended a Mini-Con together. He wouldn't agree to dress up, but he did pose for pictures and only went all '*me Tarzan, you Jane*' on her one time the whole day. *Are we dating-dating?* Even though they'd had the dating talk during their first lunch outing, they weren't moving quite as fast as she would have expected given their chemistry. They did things couples did together, but they also did things platonic friends did together. Seriously, she wasn't sure what to make of it.

Each time he brought her home, even if he came in for a bit, he left her with warm hugs and mostly chaste kisses on the lips or cheek. The times where the kisses went more deeply, they weren't accompanied by anything more—not even heavy petting. If it weren't for the times she'd felt his erection pressing into her stomach, she would think he wasn't interested in her sexually.

The snapping of fingers in front of her face made her blink. "Stop stalling and focus. We're not leaving until I see you put in some genuine effort."

His hard voice and fierce expression prompted her to square her shoulders in defiance. *Why is he acting like this?* Usually, he only watched her run drills and discussed additions to her workout with Henry.

Lifting a single eyebrow, he beckoned her forward, "***I*** know what you can do. ***You*** know what you can do. Stop over thinking it and ***show me***."

Starting her dribble again, she moved to advance around him to the right. The move was half-hearted at best, and he quickly cut her off. The deep scowl on his face made him look like one of the fearless warriors from which he was descended. A samurai through and through.

Maintaining her dribble, she backed away. Kari attempted to go to the left, but was met with a solid wall of muscle. *Shit! He's faster than he looks.* Not able to stop quickly enough, her body bumped into his and bounced off like a ping-pong ball. The basketball went flying and her body greeted the floor—butt first. Allowing herself a moment, she sat on the floor wincing at what she knew would become a bruise on her bum.

Daisuke stood above her with one hand extended, offering to help her from the floor. "Every time you go left, expect to land exactly where you are now."

Until he said it, she thought her bouncing off him was her fault. It wasn't. He'd knocked her on her ass intentionally. Ignoring his outstretched hand, her eyes full of fire, she hefted herself from the floor.

Holding her hands up to Henry, she silently called for the ball. Heart pounding in her ears, she battled with herself to move past the imagined pain and fear threatening to lock up her limbs. Propelling herself forward, she made a stronger move to her right, attempting a stop-and-pop jumper. As soon as the ball left her fingers, she knew the shot wouldn't make it anywhere near the basket. Daisuke was right there, swatting it from the air like it was an annoying gnat.

Giving herself a moment, she slowly jogged to retrieve the ball. It was hard not to allow the continued failure to take root. *Get your head right, woman! You've smoked players twice as fast as him.*

Completely healed...

That's what Dr. Mitchell told her after the last MRI. According to the trio of doctors, she should be able to function within at least ninety-five percent of her previous performance level. She and Henry had been running drills and simulation workouts for over a week. The slow-moving limp from weeks prior was non-existent. Time on the treadmill reacquainted her with her stride, but this wasn't the treadmill.

The moment she took a step with a thought to drive to the basket or the intention to square up for a jump shot, flashes of the injury-causing collision bombarded her mind. The sickening popping feeling and resulting pain were forced to the front of her brain, making it difficult to move with the ease she'd had for years prior.

Sluggishly bouncing the ball, Kari moved back toward the center of the full-sized basketball court. Henry stood on the side, arms folded, expression unreadable. Daisuke stood at the arc of the three-point line, feet wide, and arms dangling at his side.

Sweating even more profusely than she was earlier in her workout, Kari wiped her face with the tail of her shirt and took a deep draw from a water bottle. Despite not having the proper gear to play basketball, Daisuke was more than holding his own. She'd made more headway, but he continued to thwart her attempts. His body, seemingly relaxed, was poised and ready to attack her next move.

"You're still not giving one hundred percent," he rumbled. "You're too slow moving to the basket and you're barely getting off the floor with your jumper. Move past your fear. Trust yourself. If you refuse to push through this moment, you might as well retire. Call Team USA and tell them not to hold your spot on the Olympic team. You're done."

Hard eyes seized hers, rooting her in place.

"Physically, you're completely healed. The rest is all in your head. Turn off the doubt...Show me you still want it!"

Words of anger and denial leapt into her throat, but she swallowed them. She had to. He was right. Fear was controlling her. Doubt was eating away at her confidence. The whisper of thought that her final moments as a professional athlete had been spent with her on the floor thrashing in pain turned her stomach.

Memories from a previous conversation with Daisuke invaded her brain. They were talking about their families and discussing the undeniable threads of the warrior spirit present in both their blood lines.

"What do you want, Kichōna?" he queried.

"I want full control of my body back. I want to win Olympic gold one more time. And... I want one more season with my teammates."

"If that's what you want, then you'll have to fight for it. Draw on the warrior spirit of your ancestors. Allow their fierceness in the fight to overcome bondage, and their determination to maintain their lands and govern themselves, to guide you. You have their blood pumping in your veins. Your recovery isn't a mountain, Shi no shin. It's a speed bump. You just have to believe you can conquer it and you will."

Watching Daisuke standing there poised to defend the territory he'd claimed as his own, she felt a spark ignite within her. *He's standing there like this court is his. It isn't. This court is **mine**. **Any** court I set foot on belongs to me.*

Disregarding the aches in her limbs and buttocks, she pressed forward with a newfound resolve. The goal before her was clear. Make J. Daisuke Sano eat her dust. Remind him who she was.

Tossing aside her water bottle, she scooped up the basketball. Dribbling in place, she made a sharp move to the left, before quickly stepping back to the right, leaping into the air and releasing a perfect jumper. Daisuke had fully committed to the move left, so he could only watch the ball sail over his head, swishing through the net. *Once a shooter, always a shooter. Damn... That felt good.*

"Yeah! That's what I'm talking about!"

Henry yelled enthusiastically, clapping his hands and pumping his fist. When the ball rolled in his direction, he grabbed it, passing it back to her.

"Do it again."

Deftly catching the ball, she began to move with sureness, picking

Daisuke apart. His athletic past was no match for her skills. Although he knew which way she was going, she treated him to the ankle breaking moves she'd perfected over the course of her career. She exploded to the goal, speeding by him, in many cases leaving him able to do nothing more than watch her sink basket after basket. Finally, he called a halt to the workout.

"I think that's enough for today." He conceded.

Grabbing a towel from a nearby rack, he tossed one to her and wiped his face with another. At some point during the session, he'd removed his shirt. Try as she might, she couldn't ignore the play of muscles in his arms and back. Now that he wasn't her opponent, her senses had returned to her physical awareness of him as a man she found extremely attractive.

Giving her an approving pat on the back, Henry reminded her, "Don't forget, you owe me twenty laps in the pool before you leave today."

At her groan, he added, "You can thank JD for extending your time. I was going to send you to the pool forty-five minutes ago."

Leaving Daisuke and Kari alone, he exited the court through the door leading back to the office area.

"You heard the man. Time to hit the pool." Gesturing toward the door opposite to the one Henry used, he prodded, "After you, my queen."

She grabbed her duffle bag and preceded him through the opening.

Chapter Eight

KARI

It's not that she hated swimming. Strictly speaking, she loved to swim. Today, she dreaded it. After the strenuous workout with both Henry and Daisuke, her arms were leaden, and her legs were rubbery. Twenty laps felt like one hundred. The only bright spot was the refreshingly cool water flowing over her overheated body.

So focused on completing her laps, she didn't hear the splash of another body entering the pool. It wasn't until she touched the side of the pool, for the final time, that she realized she wasn't alone in the water. Once she locked onto the other person sharing the space, her eyes greedily roamed over his muscular physique, in fitted bathing trunks, as he glided through the water cutting the surface in a freestyle stroke.

The pool was just shy of Olympic sized, and wasn't nearly as deep. When she placed her feet on the bottom, the water only reached the top of her shoulders. Completing one more lap, Daisuke came to a stop on the same end of the pool, but several feet away from her.

Pushing his goggles to the top of his head, he closed the distance between them.

"How do you feel?"

Finally reaching her, he plucked a wet tendril of hair from her face and tucked it behind her ear. He kept his warm palm pressed to the side of her face, four fingers shoved gently into her wet curls, his thumb stroking her cheek.

"Tired... but oddly... good. Does that make sense?" Unconsciously, she tipped her head into his caress.

Nodding his head, he moved his other hand to her waist, drawing her closer to him.

"It's the endorphins. The rush from the feeling of accomplishment —pushing yourself to the absolute limit. You crossed a major hurdle today. I'm proud of you, *Shi no shin*."

Closing the remaining distance between them, he dipped his head taking her lips with his.

This kiss wasn't like the others. **Not. At. All.** There was absolutely nothing chaste about the way he dominated her, delving his tongue into her mouth, twirling, stroking, and driving her insane. *It should be illegal for someone to be such an amazing kisser. How did he even learn to kiss like this? Did he take a class? Was there some kind of 'Give a Woman an Orgasm with Only a Kiss' seminar? Damn...* Kari was **not** ready.

~

DAISUKE

Pressing her back into the side of the pool, he aligned his body with hers. Wearing a functional one piece *Speedo*, he knew she didn't set out to be sexy. She was though. *Very sexy.* He loved the silky feel of her soft skin beneath his calloused hands. Her body was a mixture of firm muscles and plush curves. *How is that even possible? She's driving me out of my fucking mind.*

Using both hands, he explored her body from head to thighs, stopping to tweak her nipples before reaching around and grabbing her ample bottom. He squeezed the cheeks forcing her center closer to his straining shaft. Long legs encircled his waist as if on autopilot. Neither the coolness of the water, nor the barrier of their swimwear, kept him from feeling the heat coming from her core.

Shit! He needed to stop. He'd only planned to give her a quick kiss, but his mouth had stopped listening to him. Then his hands rebelled. His legs joined the mutiny, moving him as close to her as he could get without being inside her. Drawing on an inner strength he didn't realize he possessed, Daisuke pulled away from their heated kiss. His lips finally complied. Sort of. He couldn't stop them from gently pecking her pillow soft lips a few more times before pulling away.

Groaning, he dropped his forehead to hers.

"This isn't the place for this. We need to stop."

Chocolate met hazel as he watched her eyes try to focus. Heavy breaths caused both of their chests to rapidly rise and fall. Still holding her generous globes in his hands, he set her away from his body.

"We should go."

It wasn't a suggestion. If they didn't leave now, he was positive he'd completely lose it and they'd end up making love for the first time in the pool. He couldn't do that to her. The pool was essentially a public place. Besides the fact he'd never hear the end of it from Raph and Henry, they needed privacy. Lots of it.

Sending up a prayer of thanks for having the forethought to make dinner plans with her tonight, Daisuke hustled her from the pool into the changing area. *Is it wrong to give thanks for the prospect of finally getting to make love to my woman? Possibly...Probably...Whatever.*

Somehow, he managed to convince her to shower at home. He may have used a few drugging kisses and made promises to handle dinner while she bathed and took care of her hair. Being a man of his word, he'd make sure they didn't starve. In any case, they'd need the nourishment. If he had his way, they were going to burn a massive amount of calories that would need to be replenished. They would definitely have dinner. *After.* After he'd had a chance to explore every inch of her delicious body.

Walking her to her car, he licked his lips at the prospect of tasting more of her sweetness. Pilfering one last kiss, he tapped the top of her SUV and closed the door. Once he'd seen her exit the lot safely, he hurried to his truck to follow.

Speed limits were just a suggestion and he arrived at her house minutes before her, despite her head start. He didn't want her to have too much time to over think and start questioning things. Threadbare restraint was holding the monster within him at bay. For Daisuke, his desire for Kari was always brimming just below the surface. Tonight, the dream would become reality.

Parking his truck in the extra space in her garage, he cut the engine. The door came down, closing their two vehicles into the space. By the time he rounded the front of his vehicle, she was standing at the door. Walking up behind her, he couldn't resist dropping a kiss in the space where her neck and shoulder joined. Her breath hitched, and his lips stretched into a pleased grin.

Hands lightly gripping her waist, he followed her into the mudroom. Throwing a glance over her shoulder, she pulled away and informed him, "I'm going to hop in the shower and wash this chlorine out of my hair."

Trapping her with his smoldering eyes, he advanced on her. Before she made it two steps, he snaked an arm around her, and settled her plush curves against his frame. The words forming on her lips were silenced when Daisuke pressed his lips to hers. Slipping his hands beneath her shirt, he began divesting her of her clothes—all the while moving them toward her bedroom.

If he had to recount the moments prior to them finding themselves plastered against one another in the shower, Daisuke would only be able to give their starting location and current location. They began in the mudroom and they were presently pressed together in the shower with steaming water pelting his back. They'd rushed through the actual bathing process and were now passionately entangled.

Her body was even more beautiful than he'd imagined. Not in the extra thin, sculpted way society seemed to idolize, but in the way of a woman who was unapologetically athletic, curvy and feminine. The three were not mutually exclusive. Kari was living proof.

With both hands filled with her voluptuous breasts, he admired their fullness. The contrasts between their skin tones were much more of a turn on than he could ever have anticipated. The sight of his tawny tan fingers against the lustrous brown skin of her breasts made his dick throb and his mouth water.

Enjoying the visual smorgasbord, he licked his lips.

"You are so beautiful, *Shi no shin*...I bet you taste even better than you look."

Unable to resist, he seized a dark pebbled nipple, tugging the turgid peak into his mouth. The moans and gasps floating from her lips to his ears, fueled his drive to please her. When she delved her fingers into his hair massaging his scalp, lightning shot through his pulsing shaft. She'd found his spot with the accuracy of a heat-seeking missile. Grabbing her hands, he secured them over her head. He was too close to the edge to allow her to continue her exploration.

Gliding one hand down her body, he slipped his fingers between her legs to stroke her plump folds. The slickness that greeted his fingertips definitely wasn't from the water. Thinking of sliding into her slick, warm heat pulled an involuntary groan from his throat.

"Mmm... you feel amazing, Baby."

Slipping one finger into her tight channel, he sought the little bundle of nerves with his thumb and begin to rub. Her breath hitched, and her body shook in response. Sensing she wouldn't last long this way, he added another finger and curved them inside her moist walls in a *'come here'* motion. With his digits moving deep inside her core, he used the heel of his palm to stimulate the sensitive bud of her clit. Swirling hips met his hand, and her deep moans bounced off the shower walls.

Resuming his worship of her breasts, he felt her canal grip his fingers and her body attempted to fold itself as she found her release. Liberating the nipple, he lifted his head. Daisuke didn't want to miss a moment of her climax.

Roaming eyes drank in her every response, committing them to memory. Aside from the sharp gasps and moans, his *Kichōna* was a quiet lover. Not overly vocal, but still very responsive. *Let's see if we can change that.* He wanted words added to her other displays of pleasure.

As her shivers calmed, he brought his exploring fingers to his mouth, licking them like a man long denied his favorite treat. Dark hooded eyes ensnared hers.

"Later, you can sit on my face while I sample your sweetness directly from the source."

The only response he received to his declaration was a sharp inhale and widened eyes. Reaching behind him, he turned off the spray of

69

water. Grabbing a towel, he quickly dried her then himself. He wanted all of her shivers to be due to his actions and not because he rushed her to bed wet from a shower.

No time was wasted as they moved into the bedroom, falling to the bed in a tangle of limbs. Before he lost himself completely, Daisuke grabbed condoms from the bag he'd dropped by the door and quickly covered himself.

As much as he wanted to be inside her bare, he wouldn't risk getting her pregnant. Not now. Not when she was working so hard to pursue her professional dreams. The imagined possibility of his seed growing within her made his dick hard enough to drive nails.

His *Kichōna* may be a quiet lover, but she wasn't an apathetic one. Meeting him halfway onto the bed, she initiated a toe curling kiss filled with promise. Falling back on the bed with him on top, her eager hands rubbed across his chest, wrapping around his back before latching onto his ass—squeezing and caressing his firm cheeks. The motion of her hips seemed to seek his straining dick, and he couldn't wait another moment to sink into her heated sex.

Balancing on one arm, he gripped his erection, rubbing the rounded head along her labia teasing her clit before notching it at her opening. Easing into her slowly, his eyes slammed shut at the sensation.

"Fuck!"

He growled, fighting the urge to ram his hips into hers—penetrating her core in one swift stroke.

"Ah!... Don't tease, Baby. I want to feel all of you," she moaned. Her fingers curled, pressing her nails into his back.

The stimulation was too much, and he plunged into her. Not coming to a stop until the base of his dick was swallowed by her depths —his balls resting on her ass. The suddenness seemed to steal her breath.

Daisuke couldn't help the smirk that took over his face, "Is that too much for you, Baby? You said you wanted to feel all of me."

He followed his taunt with a few shallow strokes before finding his rhythm. "Gonna fuck you hard now, *Kichōna*," he lowered his head snarling into her ear.

Shifting her left leg to his shoulder, he swerved his hips seeking that special spot he'd found in the shower. A tell-tale gasp, followed by a torrent of incoherent words, let him know he was exactly where he needed to be. Her walls clamped down on his shaft, milking him, and quiet Kari disappeared. In her place was a woman spitting out obscenities and guttural moans.

He followed her over the edge, reaching his own orgasm with choppy, spastic jerks of his hips, shooting his release into the condom covering his still rock hard dick. Not wanting the moment to end just yet, he let go of her leg and rolled to his back, pulling her on top—still impaled on his thick rod.

Pushing her hair from her face, her hands folded on his chest, she rested her chin on top of them.

"I'm not sure how you normally do friendship –"

Interrupting her quickly, he cut off a sentence he never wanted her to complete, "*Shi no shin*, if you still think we're only friends, you haven't been paying attention. I told you what I wanted. None of it has changed."

Grasping her face with both hands, his eyes bore into hers. Daisuke's voice filled with emotion and laced with steel; he spoke the words he'd been holding back for fear of overwhelming her.

"When I call you '*my queen*', it's not meaningless, nor is it a joke. I mean it exactly as I say it, because you are **my queen.** You have been, from the moment we met."

Tears threatened to spill from her eyes. Swiping at them with his thumbs, he continued.

"You are the most important person in my life. Everything, every term of endearment, or pet name has meaning."

Stroking the sides of her face, he explained, "*Kichōna* is the Japanese word for *precious*. Sweetheart...You are precious to me. You are also my *Shi no shin*, the Japanese words meaning *heart*."

Placing a gentle kiss on her lips, he carried on, laying his heart at her feet.

"Until I met you, I thought I knew what I wanted. I thought I knew my purpose. I was wrong. From the moment you said '*hello*', you have been my purpose. You are mine, *Shi no shin*. And as much as you are mine, I am yours. I love you, now and forever."

The words were barely out of his mouth before her lips came

crashing down on his in a devouring kiss. He began to harden inside her again, and her hips started to stir against his. Before they lost themselves completely, he reluctantly pulled away from the passionate kiss, his eyes searching hers.

"*Kichōna*, does this mean you feel the same way? I've laid everything out, but you haven't told me how you feel."

Tracing the lines of his face, she smiled into his eyes, "Daisuke, I love you so much it scares me. I tried to tell myself, it was all physical attraction, but I knew it wasn't true. I *never* let anyone take over, or boss me around the way I've allowed you to bulldoze your way into my life."

"I wouldn't call it bulldozing." He objected.

"It was totally bulldozing," Kari's voice was full of amusement. "You straight bullied Dr. Cotton and totally took control after my injury. Barging your way into my house, you made me drink that nasty kale smoothie. You claimed it was just because I cancelled therapy –"

"It was!" He insisted.

"Whatever you say..." The crooked smirk on her face said she didn't agree.

"Even if I am bossy, you like it," Daisuke challenged her to disagree. Two large hands landed on her round ass and squeezed.

"Maybe..." she dragged out the word, lowering her eyelids, hiding her hazel orbs from his view.

"Not maybe. Definitely."

Grabbing two hands full of her derriere, he pressed her down while flexing his hips up. Reminding her of their current position and putting an end to any coherent conversation.

A quick condom change later, and he positioned her facing away from him, kneeling on the bed with her beautiful ass on display. Sliding inside her sweet heat using one smooth thrust, he set an almost rough rhythm. The way she undulated her hips and pressed back against him, let Daisuke know she approved of the pace and wanted more. Knowing the following day was Saturday gave him a surge of delight, because he planned to gorge himself on her well into the night. Kari would get very little rest, if he had anything to do with it.

Chapter Nine

KARI

Fingers formed fists, flexed, then released at Kari's side. It was the moment of truth. Would the work she put in with the doctors at HJR pay off? Outside, the air had a cooler bite, Fall was in full season complete with multi-colored leaves falling from the trees. Inside, the chill bumps on Kari's arms defied the warmer conditioned air.

In the weeks following her breakthrough, she'd enlisted the help of a few of her teammates to turn her workouts into real scrimmages. Facing off against Daisuke and Henry was a good start, but her ability to best either of them wasn't an accurate measure of her readiness for competition.

They were both in great physical shape, but neither had played competitive sports since college, over fifteen years ago. Which meant they weren't in playing shape and didn't possess the speed and endurance she required to accurately test her progress and assess what was still needed.

The willingness of her teammates to give up several hours a week to scrimmage with her warmed Kari's heart. As team captain, she'd always tried to be a person others were happy to follow as well as the kind of leader who inspired those around her to step up whenever they were needed.

Looking around at the ladies assembled on the *Fantasy* practice court, she could say with confidence, she had done her job as captain well. Every member of her team was present, even though only two others were actual members of Team USA women's basketball.

Silence reigned among them while Team USA head coach, Alex Williams-Cherry, stood on the side of the court speaking with her staff. Making eye contact with each of her teammates, Kari signaled for them to bring it in to a huddle.

Once they were linked in a circle, their arms thrown around one another's shoulders, she expressed her gratitude.

"Thank you all for being here to support me. Y'all have gone above and beyond, and I sincerely appreciate it. I wouldn't be here, if it weren't for each and every one of you. You have no idea how much it means to me to have you here."

Tears clogged her throat, making the last of her words come out in a shaky whisper.

"Come on, Queen. You know we gotchu," Kelly bumped Kari's hip with her own, a watery smile plastered on her face.

The rest of her teammates chimed in, echoing Kelly's statement with their own words of encouragement. Without thinking they moved into their pregame ritual. No, this wasn't an actual game, but the stakes were just as high for Kari as they had been during the championship game over the summer.

Rocking their bodies from side to side to a rhythm only they could hear, they got into the flow of the routine. Drawing strength from her teammates, Kari yelled out the first question, "What are we?"

"We are Unstoppable!"

"What do we do?"

"Dominate!"

"*What* do we do?!"

"Annihilate!"

"Whose court is this?"

"Ours!"

"**Whose** court is *this*?"

"OURS!"

"That's right! This is our court!"

The familiarity of the ritual jump started her adrenaline. Feeding off the intensity of her teammates, she asked the final question. "What time is it?"

"It's time to go to work!"

"Damn right it is! Let's do this!"

Skip-stepping in front of each woman in the circle, she slapped high fives and handed out enthusiastic fist bumps. Moving to the center, she raised a single fist in the air, calling them in closer without the use of words. Twelve other hands raised along-side hers, some touching hers, overlapping, stacking, and holding on to one another.

In the final part of the custom, she yelled out, "On three! One, two, three!"

Simultaneously, they yelled, "Go to work!"

Patting one another on the back, they broke out of the huddle, moving into their designated positions on the court. Having watched them from the sideline, Coach Williams-Cherry asked for twenty minutes on the clock and blew her whistle to start the scrimmage.

For the ensuing twenty minutes, Kari's teammates did exactly what she'd asked of them. They played as if there was another championship on the line. Since they knew all her moves, they challenged her, pushing her to her limits.

Chest heaving, with sweat dripping from her chin, Kari stood just outside the three-point arc in a face-off with Fredricka. Being the fastest and one of their best defenders, Freddy was the obvious choice to guard her. Angling her body away, she moved the ball just out of Freddy's reach, narrowly avoiding the swiping hand of her teammate.

Always aware of the time, she knew there were roughly forty-five seconds left on the clock. The parallel between this match up and the one from the title game didn't escape Kari's notice, but she pushed past the fleeting moment of anxiety.

Holding up her left arm, she called the play. The rest happened as it should have during that fateful game. She passed the ball and cut through the paint, hitting the back corner and popping back up to the right side of the basket just in time to catch the return pass.

Quickly dribbling to her left, she led her defender right to Kelly's screen. Two quick bounces past the screen, she got a look at the basket, elevated and released the ball. The shot swished through the net and Kari landed on two feet with a whoop of relief.

The buzzer sounded signaling the end of the scrimmage and her teammates converged on her, jumping in excitement. She felt like herself for the first time in months. Once the exhilaration of the moment passed, her teammates wished her luck and filed off the court, heading to the locker room.

Their exit left her alone with Coach Williams-Cherry and her assistants. The coach took a few long, unnerving moments in quiet conversation with her assistants before turning and calling Kari over to them, "How do you feel?"

Smiling broadly, Kari responded, "I feel great! Like myself again."

"Well, you moved and played a hell of a lot better than I expected coming off an ACL injury. Those guys at HJR may be miracle workers, but I know you put serious time into getting over the hump."

Nodding in acknowledgement, Kari tried not to fidget as she waited anxiously for the coach to let her know if she was impressed enough to at least keep her name on the team roster. She managed to keep her hands still, but she nervously shifted from one foot to the other,

"I'm not going to keep you in suspense. I'd be a fool not to offer to keep you on the team as starting point guard. The way you're playing, I can already feel the weight of another gold medal around my neck."

Kari beamed under the praise from the legendary coach. "Thank you so much, Coach! I promise, you won't regret taking a chance on me." She grasped the coach's hand, shaking it vigorously.

"I don't see a risk in keeping you on, Queen. You know I don't sugar coat and I don't say things I don't mean. Keep your regimen up and I'll see you at the next practice. Coach Jackson will send you all the info."

Having given her decision, the coach picked up her belongings and walked away—her assistants following closely behind.

Kari watched the coach's retreating back until she cleared the exit. Thankful to be alone, she released an excited squeal. Twirling in a circle and jumping excitedly, she held a one woman celebration.

"Careful, *Kichōna*. We wouldn't want to undo all of our hard work now, would we?"

Daisuke's voice startled her, stopping her mini-celebration mid squeal. Whirling around, she eyed him in surprise.

"How long have you been standing there?"

His stealthy mannerisms could be more than a bit unnerving. Hearing a voice behind you, without any warning steps, can scare the bejesus out of a person.

Glancing at his watch, Daisuke feigned calculating in his head. "Five minutes... Give or take twenty-five." Grinning widely, he wrapped her in his arms and hugged her tightly, giving her the feeling of being surrounded by his love.

"I'm proud of you, *Shi no shin*. You were amazing. I knew you were ready. You've proven you're just as good, if not better than you were before."

Dropping a drugging kiss on her lips, he murmured, "What do you say we go back to my place? I'll help you relax with a nice hot shower... Maybe a full body massage..."

He pressed his hips forward suggestively and Kari knew exactly what kind of *full body massage* he was offering.

"I –"

Kari's next words were cut off by whistles, yells and whoops. Without looking, she knew who was behind the interruption. A quick glance confirmed her suspicions. Kelly, Terri and Freddy were standing in the opening leading onto the court from the locker room.

"Really mature, ladies. Really mature."

Her attempt at chastising them was wasted energy. Kelly propped her chin on folded hands and made doe eyes at the two of them, blinking rapidly. *I guess she's supposed to be batting her eyelashes.*

Not to be left out, Terri was making kissing noises and Freddy was doing a truly awful running man. How that fit into the situation, Kari had no clue, but it was the straw that broke the camel's back. She held on to Daisuke's arms laughing so hard, she almost doubled over.

"Bye! Get lost, crazy ladies!" She managed to squeeze out between bouts of laughter.

Instead of leaving, they moved closer to her and Daisuke. His arms were still locked around her waist, holding her firmly. By sheer force of habit, her hands were on him as well. Their cozy embrace didn't go unnoticed.

"What's up, Doc?"

Ever the spokeswoman, Kelly was the first to actually greet Daisuke. Terri and Freddy parroted Kelly's greeting. Smiling indulgently, he returned their greeting with a short hello.

"So..." Terri began, her eyes sweeping over the two of them. "Do y'all have something you want to tell us?"

Her brow furrowed in mock confusion, Kari answered Terri's question with a question of her own. "Such as?"

"See...You're standing here acting brand new. You're gonna make us go there, huh?" Kelly jumped in to assist Terri in operation *'Get in Kari's Business.'*

"Keep playing and I'll tell him what you used to call him," Kelly warned.

"Kelly! I never called him that and you know it." Kari cast a furtive glance at Daisuke as she defended herself.

"If you never said it, how do you know what she's talking about?" Freddy chimed in, wiggling her eyebrows at Kari and grinning smugly.

"Please don't," Kari pleaded.

Though they never attempted to keep their relationship a secret, she and Daisuke hadn't made a formal announcement of their couple status. That was the admission her teammates wanted. They wanted her to admit she and Daisuke were together, and they'd been right all along about how the two of them felt about one another.

Pleading hazel eyes met his soft brown orbs. Either he misread her expression, or he didn't care, because he dropped a soft kiss on her lips and whispered in her ear.

"When we get home, we'll discuss this nickname you failed to mention having for me."

He punctuated his statement with a light tap to her butt. Raising his head, he looked at her teammates.

"Ladies, as much as we would love to stay and hang out with you, I promised my queen a nice hot shower and a celebratory massage."

Jaw hanging open in shock, she stared at Daisuke in disbelief. "That doesn't help this situation, sir. Not at all."

Ignoring her comments and the good natured jeering from her friends, he steered her toward the locker room to gather her things. Along the way, his voice rumbled in her ear with descriptions of the things he had in store for her. Desire crawled up her spine and spiraled down to her center. She was very much looking forward to him keeping every single promise. Not just for that night, but every night to come. Smiling at him seductively, she thought of all the delicious perks to being *Sano's Queen*.

Epilogue

KARI

Tokyo, Japan Summer 2020

The house lights were dimmed. Strobe lights danced around the enormous space, bouncing through the crowd. The noise from the thousands of people gathered was deafening. The thrumming baseline of popular hip hop beats blasted through the arena.

Overhead, the *Jumbotron* displayed the images of four members of the starting line-up for Team USA Women's Basketball, standing at center court. Their elevated energy visible in the high fives and slaps to the backs of their teammates. They were ready to complete the journey to acquire the seventh consecutive Olympic Gold medal for the United States Women's basketball program.

The booming voice of the announcer blasted through the massive facility as he introduced the Team USA starters. "Aaaannnd now, the 5'9" point guard from the *Atlanta Fantasy* by way of Henry Johnson University, a three-time Olympic Gold Medalist, going for her fourth – NUMBER TWENTY-TWO. KARI, THE QUEEEEN, SAAAANOOOO!

Springing from her seat, Kari sprinted into the spotlight to meet her teammates at the center of the basketball court. Moving about the huddle, she accepted and delivered high fives, fist bumps and back slaps. Her adrenaline and her spirits were high as she took in the expressions on the faces of the women who would join her in the quest to once again bring honor to the sport and the USA Women's program.

When they broke from the huddle, Kari's eyes cut to the sideline. Standing at the end of the bench with the medical staff was Daisuke. Her new husband met her gaze with the fiery resolve of a warrior. Legs spread shoulder width apart, broad shoulders squared, his arms extended with his hands fisted together as if he held his ancestor's Samurai sword. She mirrored the pose; her face a mask of determination. Receiving a nod of affirmation from her life mate, she released the pose. Moving with purposeful strides, she joined her teammates gathered around the coach. *It was time to go to work.*

The End

Coming Soon

Continue reading for a sneak peek at the upcoming novel scheduled to release fall 2022

INVOLUNTARY

Chapter One

STEPHANIE

Please God. Please let my baby be okay. Rushing through the security check point at the ER entrance, my hands were shaking so badly I could hardly empty my pockets like the security guard requested. My heart was pounding so loud, I could barely hear anything being said to me. Finally, I get through the security check. My cousin Gene wasn't far behind me, taking his turn at the security check point. Thank God he was at the salon when I got the call. The way I'm feeling, I would have ended up in an accident trying to get here.

There's a lone woman sitting at a desk behind the glass separator as I walked into to reception area. Reading the Registrar nameplate; I hurriedly approach the glass. I glimpsed the badge pinned to the collar of the woman's scrubs–Charlotte Wright. The ER is crowded, but I say a prayer of thanks there's no line at the registrar's desk. All the nerves in my body screamed at me to get to Saffi. I know the woman heard me approach. I saw her look up then back at her computer screen. Using every ounce of self-control I can muster, I stood quietly at the desk waiting. And waiting.

Charlotte was typing away on the computer as though I wasn't standing less than five feet in front of her, separated only by the desk and protective glass. It was probably only a couple of minutes, but it felt like hours. *This is some bullshit.* Rapping my knuckles against the counter, I attempted to get her attention.

"Excuse me, ma'am. Can you help me? I got a call that my daughter was here," I promise I tried to sound as nice as my frayed nerves would allow.

Charlotte stopped typing, and gave me a sour expression as if I inconvenienced her by expecting her to actually do her job. I don't have time for her bullshit, so I gave her my, *get off your ass and do your job,* look.

"If you will give me a minute, I'll be right with you." Her words weren't rude, but her tone and facial expression were a whole other matter. *This chick is testing me.* I'm trying hard not to be *that* person. The person who cuts up and curses people in service jobs out, but this is a damn emergency room. She could at least pretend she understood her environment.

I opened my mouth, but Gene placed a hand on my shoulder. I looked up to see him shaking his head at me. Moving me gently to the side, he moved closer to the desk. He knows I don't play when it comes to Saffi. If I have to wait on something dealing with me, I'm cool, but not when it comes to her.

"Ma'am, we don't mean to rush you, but my little cousin is here. She's only twelve years old. She was attacked and she's probably scared out her mind right now."

Motioning to me, he gave her his charming best. "My little cousin's name is Chloe Barker. This is her mother, Stephanie. Can you help us?"

There was no other way to describe my cousin Gene other than to say he's a beautiful black man. Tall, with broad shoulders that tapered down at his waist and hips, he constantly drew attention. His physique is packed with thick, sculpted, muscle. The dark brown skin wrapping his frame glowed with good health and his full lips are outlined with a well-maintained goatee. Upon first meeting him, his overall appearance tended to strike the unsuspecting person dumb—women and men alike.

Apparently, Charlotte was no exception. The fingers tapping away at the keyboard stopped moving and her pale green eyes unglued themselves from the computer screen to view the source of the deep, raspy voice with a touch of country boy thrown in. Hungry eyes raked over the parts of Gene not obscured by the half-wall, and her cheeks flushed pink.

"Of course, I can! Let me just check the admissions log," She smiled at him, damn near showing all thirty-two of her teeth. "You say her name is Chloe Barker?"

Only concentrating really hard on my baby kept me from telling her about her fake, horny ass. *I'm not like this... I swear I'm not.* Most of the time, I'm told I'm too nice and give people too many chances, but this trick was begging to meet the hood chick I kept tucked away.

"Shh, cuz. I gotchu," Gene whispered, patting me on the back. I needed to give him a raise. He might have just saved me from jail, because I could NOT with this person right now. As a hair stylist and business owner, service was my life's blood. People in service jobs, who are crappy at it and obviously don't want to do it, were a trigger for me. Taking a deep breath, I tried to keep calm. *Focus on Saffi. You can't help her from the back of a squad car.*

Charlotte was super helpful—when Gene was the one asking. I didn't miss the way she sat up taller in her chair, flipping her blonde hair and tugging on her scrub top making it stretch tighter across the nubs passing for breasts on her chest. *I know it was petty thought, but I couldn't help it.* Anything she did aside from getting me to my baby was annoying the shit out of me.

"Oh!" Lifting wide eyes from the computer screen, she looked from Gene's face to mine. "It says here that her mother, Danielle, arrived with her." Her face pinched in irritation, because I guess she thought Gene was lying to her.

He wasn't lying. Legally, Saffi is **my** daughter—even if Dani did give birth to her. She's never taken care of Saffi, leaving her first with my grandmother. My grandmother helped me adopt Saffi officially before she passed away. So, no matter what Dani said, Saffi is my child.

"I'm afraid I can't let you go back. There's only one visitor allowed and her mother is already with her," The way her eyes twinkled almost gleefully, said she wasn't sorry at all to deny me access.

"Ma'am, I don't care what that woman said. **I** am Chloe Sophia

Barker's mother. **Not** her," I was pissed beyond belief and ready to burst through the doors searching every room individually.

Shaking off Gene's hand of caution, I continued, "Saffi has been to this hospital before, when she had appendicitis. If you will check your records, you will see the name of her parent is listed as Stephanie Barker, *me*, *not* Danielle Barker."

I was adamant, but I didn't raise my voice. It was a constant struggle to maintain my composure, because all I could think about was how frightened Saffi must be. By now, a line had begun to form behind myself and Gene. Flicking her eyes between us, Charlotte took note of the growing queue.

"Look, I don't know what else to tell you. From this entry, her mother is already with her. There can only be one person at time in the treatment area, so you'll have to wait or call Ms. Barker and ask her to come out so you can go in. Now, if you'll step aside, I need to help the person behind you." she snipped.

Aw hell naw! "No Charlotte. I will not step aside," my voice rising in volume, I again shrugged off Gene's attempts to calm me.

"Listen, I'm not sure what is going on to make you first ignore me, then not even have the courtesy of looking to verify the accuracy of information I'm giving you, but I've had enough. I want to see my child, and I want to see her RIGHT NOW!"

If I had the type of skin that more easily showed my moods, my face would have been beet red. As it was, I felt like I was being heated from within like a boiler, and steam was coming out of my ears.

Charlotte's entire face closed up; her lips pinched so tightly together her mouth looked like a sphincter. "Listen you –"

"Is there a problem here?" A voice cut across the comeback Charlotte was set to deliver from her intolerable face. We all turned our attention to the petite brunette approaching the registrar's desk.

"No!"

"Yes!"

Both Charlotte and I answered simultaneously. The woman must have been someone important, because Charlotte tried to fix her face. All I was thinking was, if the woman was important, maybe she could get our unfriendly registrar to do her job.

DARIE MCCOY

"I'm Princess Wells, the administrator on this shift. What seems to be the problem?" Turning to my current nemesis first, she prompted, "Charlotte, please explain."

Aw, here we go. When she allowed pinched face to speak first, I knew my chances of seeing Saffi anytime soon where going down the drain. I clenched my fists at my side and waited to hear which lie fell from her lips first.

"Well... I was just informing *these people* that only one person was allowed back in the treatment room, and since the patient they asked about already has someone in the room, they can't go back. Then, she started yelling at me. I have no idea why. I didn't make the rule," She practically whined.

Her cheeks pinkened and her eyes welled with tears. Fake ass tears, because I hadn't done anything for her to cry about. If she really wanted a reason to leak like a faucet, I could make that happen for her in two ticks or less.

Looking at Ms Wells, who wore office attire instead of scrubs, I couldn't read the expression on her face. She turned dark grey eyes to my face, expectantly. I didn't have a problem obliging the unspoken request. I very bluntly, and much more honestly, related to her the situation and the urgency for me to see Saffi.

Once I was done, her face tightened and her voice was even tighter. When she turned towards Charlotte, I just knew she was going to ask her to call security to remove me. Instead, she picked up the phone and called someone from the back to open the second desk to assist the people in line behind me. Then, she instructed Charlotte to move away from the computer and she took a seat in front of the monitor.

Relief flooded my body when she began actually doing what I'd been asking Charlotte to do all along. It's a hospital, there are laws, so I knew she had to verify the information I gave her before she could give me access. I didn't flinch when she asked for ID to confirm my identity.

Once we'd taken care of that task, she pressed the button, buzzing me through the doors. Gene was going to stay behind, but she waved him in as well. She told Charlotte she would be back to speak with her once she walked me to Saffi's room. From the way Charlotte shrank in her seat, the conversation wasn't going to be pleasant for her. *Good.*

90

"Mrs. Barker –"

"Miss"

"Miss Barker, if the woman in the room with Chloe isn't her mother, who is she?" Ms. Wells asked a legitimate question as we walked through the maze of rooms and curtained off areas.

"The woman is my sister Danielle. She's Chloe's birth mother, but I adopted Chloe when she was 5, so legally, I'm her mother," I explained.

I never wanted to deny Saffi access to Danielle, but if I found out she played a part in what happened to my baby, I was cutting Dani off completely. She was more than welcome to fuck up her own life, but I wouldn't let her put Saffi in danger.

We reached a door and Ms. Wells knocked before pushing it open. Saffi was lying prone with a woman and man in scrubs standing to either side of her. There was some kind of gauze like paper laid across her forehead and nose, covering a part of her face and hair. My heart seized in my chest and my breath caught in my throat when I saw the three long slashes on her cheek and jaw. Two of the slashes were horizontal and one was vertical.

Her clothes were tattered. One sleeve of her short-sleeved top was barely hanging on and there was blood splattered all over the front, with the majority being on her left side. There was more blood splattered on her jean shorts and the sneakers that were white when she left home this morning. My heart started thudding in my ears again. Remaining focused was a struggle, but not having a clear head wasn't an option.

I placed my attention on the man to Saffi's left. Strands of ginger hair peeked from beneath the *Star Wars* themed scrub cap he wore. He looked like he'd just finished cleaning her wounds and was reaching to a tray, for what I don't know, but I was going to find out. I didn't know if this guy was a resident, a regular ER doctor or what, but he looked really young.

Turning to Ms. Wells, I made my request before the young physician could do anything more, "Please ask him to stop what he's doing. I have questions and concerns."

She didn't ask me to explain, she just honored my request. I was grateful, because my emotions were all over the place and internally, I was on the verge of a complete come apart.

"Dr. Pearson, please stop what you're doing. This is Chloe Barker's mother, Stephanie Barker and she has questions about her condition," Ms. Wells moved farther into the room and stepped to the side to give me and Gene space.

Flicking my eyes to Danielle sitting in the lone chair in the room, I didn't miss her guilty posture. It wasn't a priority, but I'd definitely get to her once I made sure Saffi was getting the best care possible. I really wanted answers as to what happened and how it happened, but I'd have to wait for those too. *One thing at a time Steph. Saffi first. Beat Dani's ass second.*

I approached the end of the bed and touched Saffi's leg, rubbing it gently. "Dr. Pearson, are you a general physician or a specialist?"

I'd read somewhere you had a right to request a plastic surgeon for times like this and that was what I wanted for Saffi. If he wasn't a plastic surgeon, I wanted one.

"I'm the Chief ER resident on this shift, ma'am. So, I guess you could say I'm a general physician," Dr. Pearson answered, not appearing to be insulted by my question. Good because things could get sticky when I requested a plastic surgeon.

"Could you quickly explain to me your treatment plan? Are the cuts on her face deep? How were you planning to close them? Stitches? Glue?" My gaze locked on his, but I saw Dani shift in the seat from the corner of my eye.

No one asked her for her two cents, but she gave it anyway, "I told them to use glue or stitches. Whatever, just stop the bleeding."

This bitch... I know she's my sister, but sometimes... Ugh! I really wished she'd just kept her mouth shut.

"Dani, I wasn't talking to you. I was talking to Dr. Pearson. Besides, that wasn't your decision to make." I was turning back to speak to Dr. Pearson when my sister decided she wasn't done chipping in her two cents.

"Whatchu mean it's not my decision? I don't remember you laying up in the hospital for 10 hours giving birth to her," her eyes shined with malice and a hint of smugness, knowing I couldn't refute the fact she had given birth to Saffi.

I'd promised myself I wouldn't argue with Dani in front of Saffi and my sister was making it really difficult to keep that promise. No, I didn't lie in a hospital for 10 hours giving birth to Saffi, but I did get up every two hours to feed her once she came home from the hospital. I was still in college at the time, but I rearranged my class and work schedules to be available to help look after my niece.

Not one day of Saffi's life had Danielle ever actually been a mother to the child she brought into the world. A week after giving birth, Danielle up and left. She didn't say a word to anyone. She simply left. After 6 months of hearing nothing from her, my grandmother went to a social worker and started the process of becoming a foster parent, so she could have legal guardianship over Saffi. Between me and my grand-mother, all of Saffi's needs were met.

When Grandma Viola got sick, with her blessing, I went back to social services and petitioned for custody of Saffi, who was only two years old at the time. I always tried to make sure Saffi knew she was loved, and I never wanted her to feel anything other than affection for her birth mother.

No matter how much my stomach filled with knots whenever she asked to spend time with Dani, I didn't bad-mouth my sister. Yep. Saffi asked for Dani, but I could count on **one** hand the amount of times Dani had actually called and asked for Saffi. Today was one of those days and look what happened. Saffi lands in the hospital with her face cut up and Danielle couldn't care less if she ended up with permanent physical scars to go along with the emotional scars she was bound to have from this experience.

My whole body was as taunt as a bow string pulled back ready to launch an arrow. I knew where that arrow would land and how much damage it would do, so I looked at Gene, "Will you take her out of here? I can't do this with her right now."

Gene upped his cred as my favorite cousin and trusted friend, because he hustled Dani out of my sight almost as soon as the words left my mouth. Everyone ignored the parting remarks she spat out, while he bodily moved her through the door and out into the lobby. Seeing that I no longer needed her, Ms. Wells followed quietly behind them.

Focusing my attention back on Dr. Pearson, I resumed my ques-tions, "You were saying?"

The youthful doctor increased his integrity with me when he explained his treatment plan for dealing with the slashes on Saffi's face, then followed it with the options for contacting the plastic surgeon on call, which was going to be my request.

I jumped on the suggestion and asked for the plastic surgeon to be notified. I didn't care about the cost. I didn't want Saffi to look in the mirror on a daily basis and see a physical reminder of this horrific ordeal.

Dr. Pearson also informed me that they'd given her something for the pain once they confirmed she didn't have any potential allergies to the medication. From the way she was laid out, they'd done more than given her something for the pain, she appeared to be sleeping, so I asked, "Did you sedate her?"

"Yes ma'am. We had to. She was still very agitated when the paramedics brought her in and she wouldn't let us get close enough to assess her injuries. She kept calling out for Aunt Cee-Cee. I'm guessing that's you," he stared at me with kind, cinnamon colored eyes.

Thinking of Saffi crying out for me, and me not being there for her brought tears to my eyes. Clearing my throat, and swiping at the tears before they could fall, my gaze roamed over my baby's prone body taking in every detail. That's when I noticed the way her fists clenched and the grimace on the side of her face not covered by the draped cloth.

"Are the slashes on her face her only injuries? She still looks like she's in pain," my brow was crinkled in concern. *What happened to my baby girl?*

"She has some bruising on her abdomen and back, but the cuts on her face seemed to be the primary damage," Dr. Pearson was efficient, but I had a nagging feeling they missed something.

"The medicine you gave her was also for pain, right?" My eyes pinged between the doctor and the nurse still standing beside the bed. The nurse checked the chart and confirmed doctor's statement.

"So, should she still be grimacing like that? Look at her hands, the way her fists are clenched. When she had appendicitis, once they sedated her, she didn't move at all. I think there's something else wrong."

So far, Dr. Pearson had been helpful, I prayed this wouldn't be one of those times a physician failed to listen to the concerns of an African

American patient. It happened far too often and I didn't want Saffi to be a statistic.

Because of her age and current state of unconsciousness, she couldn't tell them what was going on, but my gut wouldn't let go of the idea. *Something wasn't right.* I could feel it. Dr. Pearson placed his attention on Saffi, apparently looking for the signals I'd described. It only took a few moments, of him visually inspecting her, for him to start issuing instructions to the nurse at his side.

I didn't realize I was holding my breath until I released it, along with some of the tension I was holding in my shoulders. I had to keep reminding myself that this was a good hospital, which was why I'd brought Saffi here the one other time she'd required serious medical attention.

Hyperaware of everything taking place in front of me, I immediately picked up on the change in Dr. Pearson's demeanor. He'd been gingerly pressing along Saffi's torso when he suddenly snatched the stethoscope from around his neck, putting it on. His facial expression was intense as he began placing the head of the scope in different places on her chest. Delivering short taps to her chest, he continued to listen through the device. Cursing under his breath, he snatched the headset from his ears.

"Nurse Stevenson, page Dr. Anderson, we might need him. Page Dr. Maxwell as well," Dr. Pearson directly tersely.

I could tell whatever he heard through the stethoscope was urgent, and I couldn't prevent the words tumbling from my mouth even if I'd wanted to stop them.

"What is it? What's wrong?" The pleading note of my voice was foreign to my ears, and I waited anxiously for him to explain.

With his hands efficiently placing a large gauze bandage over the injured side of Saffi's face, Dr. Pearson gave me a quick assessment, "If what I felt and heard is correct, she has a couple of cracked ribs. She's struggling a bit to breath, so I'm concerned she may have a pneumothorax. I'm going to get her upstairs for chest X-rays and I've asked for the Cardiothoracic surgeon on shift to be called to consult and operate if necessary."

"Wait! A Surgeon! Operate! What is a pneumothorax?" Frantic

didn't accurately describe how I felt listening to Dr. Pearson. I was about to come completely unglued.

Continuing to move about the small room, prepping Saffi to move, he answered my question, "In laymen's terms, a pneumothorax is a collapsed lung. Depending on how badly her ribs are injured, they could have punctured her lung, allowing air to fill the area between the chest cavity and the lung itself."

In quick strides, Nurse Stevenson bustled through the door, propping it open, just as Dr. Pearson finished readying Saffi for transport. Dismissing me to focus on their patient, they rolled her out of the room and down the corridor.

"Oh my God... Oh my God!" I was failing miserably at remaining calm. *Broken ribs! A punctured lung! What the FUCK happened to my child?* I hustled to keep up with the medical team zipping through the ER maze to the elevators. There was no way they were leaving me behind.

Chapter Two

JIAN

As I walked out of the patient's room following a routine post op check-in, I heard my name being called from the nearby nurse's station. I don't normally do post-op checks at night, but I figured if I had to be at the hospital on night shift, I might as well check in on my patients.

"Dr. Anderson, I just got a call from the ER, they have an adolescent patient with a possible pneumothorax and they've asked for a consult. Dr. Pearson has taken the patient for X-Rays to confirm. Radiology room 12," Paige Carmichael, the charge nurse, let me know as I approached the station.

Not slowing down, I flashed her a smile as I walked past her, making my way to the elevator, "Thank you Nurse Carmichael. Please let him know I'm on my way down."

I ignored the way her cheeks flushed, and I pretended not to notice she was staring at my ass while I walked away. When I was younger, I was flattered by the way women responded to me. I'm no saint. I'd partaken in the offerings from women frequently in my youth.

Quickly approaching forty, I've found that being looked at like a piece of man-meat had gotten old. Not that the attention wasn't appreciated, I'm a heterosexual man and by strict DNA coding we enjoy knowing a woman found us attractive.

The sly looks, blushes and comments increased in frequency once the *Netflix* series *Wu Assassins* became popular. The female staff spent far too much time discussing how uncanny the resemblance was between me and the actor Byron Mann, who played the character *Uncle Six* in the series. I'm slightly taller and a little heavier, but even I had to admit the similarity was there.

When I first joined the staff at Talbot Memorial, it seemed every unmarried woman in the place was looking to add me as their plus one. Either as a conquest for bragging rights, or in the hopes of becoming a surgeon's housewife. The former couldn't happen because I had a firm policy against dating or fooling around with my colleagues. The latter couldn't occur because I never understood why any person would spend years obtaining education only to give it up. All of the invitations had come from women who'd spent years in school, then additional time building their careers and reputations.

I'd asked my mother once if she regretted giving up her career to become a stay-at-home mom. Offering me an indulgent smile, she assured me she had no regrets. She said, being my mother was the most important work she'd ever done, so she was honored to be able to be there for me in that way. I accepted her words, but I didn't understand her perspective.

She'd worked hard to obtain her doctorate and was on a tenure track at her Alma Mater. Everything changed following my arrival. I'm thankful for her, for both my parents, but I couldn't fathom the sacrifices she made for me. Sacrifices she's told me repeatedly were her honor to make.

The elevator doors opened and I stepped out onto the radiology floor. Walking down the hall, I saw a woman pacing at the end with a cellphone pressed to her ear. I couldn't distinguish much of her face, since I could only see her in profile and the phone covered most of the side facing me. She spoke in hushed tones. Her free arm was wrapped under her generous bosom, while her hand tightly gripped the side of her shirt. Her entire demeanor was the definition of concerned family member. Instinctively, I redirect my course to move toward her instead of the radiology room. Before I could say anything to her, the door to room twelve opened capturing both of our attention.

The ER resident, Pearson was framed in the doorway with the radiologist and a nurse standing inside, "Great! You're here. We have the X-rays for our patient Chloe Barker."

He waved me into the room, where the radiologist immediately went over his interpretation of the X-Rays with us. As we spoke, my eyes drifted to the unconscious pre-teen lying on the gurney. I'm not sure what her complexion normally looked like, but her deeply tanned skin seemed to hold a pallor under the bandage covering half of her face. I'd heard and seen enough.

Making eye contact with the nurse, I read her name badge. "Nurse Stevenson, please book an OR equipped for the possibility of having to open the chest cavity. Hopefully, it won't come to that."

Pearson added on, "Could you also make sure Dr. Maxwell has what she needs in there as well?"

Dr. Georgina Maxwell is the best plastic surgeon on staff, possibly the best on the east coast. *Why would she join me in the ER?* "Dr. Pearson, why do we need Dr. Maxwell for a pneumothorax? She's plastics."

Motioning to the left side of his face with his hand he gave me a quick rundown about the cuts the child had sustained in addition to her other injuries. I thought my years of practice and doing my own tour of the ER as a resident all those years ago had hardened me to the things people did to one another. I guess I was wrong.

Listening to Pearson detail the patient's injuries and that her state of trauma so severe she had to be sedated, my blood started to boil. Who would do such a thing to an innocent child? Gritting my teeth, I worked to keep my anger in check.

The young physician answered my unspoken question about the woman pacing in the hallway, "Her mother, the woman in the hallway, asked for a plastic surgeon to treat the child in the hopes the wounds would heal with minimal scarring. I can't say that I blame her. I do damn good sutures, but they don't compare to Dr. Maxwell's level of precision. She does amazing work."

He was right. Georgina was a miracle worker. She was hands down one of the most gifted plastic surgeons I'd ever encountered. Waving my hand, indicating he should follow me, we stepped into the hallway to speak with Chloe's mother. We would have to make it quick; I didn't like the sounds of the child's breathing.

Since he had a rapport from meeting her in the ER, I allowed Dr. Pearson to take the lead, "Miss Barker, this is Dr. Jian Anderson. He's a cardiothoracic surgeon." Lifting a hand toward me, he didn't try to explain my role any further.

She was no longer on the phone, so I could see her entire face. Even with the puffiness around her startling black eyes from a recent crying jag, and her face devoid of make-up, she was breathtaking. *Like seriously, I quit breathing.* Her skin was a flawless canvas painted the shade of mahogany. Her full lips were pursed in a concerned pout below a button nose. She was too beautiful to be real. Against my will and good decorum, my eyes drifted from her face to sweep her frame. My eyes raked over her compact body taking in the generous curves, which made up for what she lacked in physical height. Clearing his throat, Pearson brought me back to the situation at hand.

Thankful for the nudge back into reality, I reached a hand forward to shake hers as I shifted into surgical mode. With as much clarity as possible, I explained to her what was needed, gaining her consent to perform more invasive surgery if initial treatment options weren't successful.

While we were talking, two surgical aids rolled Chloe from the room to prep her for surgery. Visually following the progress of the gurney down the hall, Miss Barker's eyes filled with tears that refused to fall and an invisible fist gripped my heart, squeezing. Unconsciously, I rubbed my chest above the malfunctioning muscle. Her obvious emotional pain was causing me physical pain and I had neither the time or willingness to delve into the reasons why.

Clasping her free hand between both of mine, I ignored how good her silky skin felt against my palms. Capturing her gaze, I spoke to her softly, "Hey... I know it's a bit scary, but let's keep a positive outlook. Your daughter is in very good hands. We will do our very best to take care of her."

I held on to her gaze and her hand until I received a nod of agreement from her. Sticking my head into the now almost vacant room, I asked the radiologist to show Miss Barker to the surgical waiting room.

Deciding Pearson's quick thinking and thoroughness deserved a reward, I tossed him a glance, "Do you want to scrub in with me?"

Before he could verbally accept, I saw the answer written across his face. Pearson was a good kid. Although he worked mostly in the ER, he was still entertaining a specialty, and I wanted to see where his head was regarding cardio. Talbot was a teaching hospital, but I was extremely selective about whom I invited into my OR. Pearson recognized the boon for the rare opportunity that it was, and quickly accepted my invitation.

Things in an operating room are unpredictable, so I always function under the thought '*expect the unexpected*'. Tonight, the *unexpected* occurrence was everything going smoothly. Although the patient's broken ribs had punctured her lung, allowing air into the chest cavity, it wasn't so severe as to require actual surgery to correct. We were able to release the pressure with needles. If the child hadn't been covered in bruises with lacerations on her face, I would say she had a guardian angel watching over her protectively, making her life a charmed one.

As if she had her ear to the door, Dr. Maxwell arrived with her resident in tow while we were placing bandages around the relief port I'd leave in for a short time, to mitigate another lung collapse. After a quick assessment of the patient's injuries, she got right down to business. I didn't have to, but I stayed to watch her work, while monitoring Chloe's vitals. I'm normally thorough, so I didn't want think too much about why I stayed.

Usually, in situations where my patient required more than just my expertise, I would step out to update the family after I was done with my portion. The only times I didn't do so was when the patient's condition was still too critical to call, without waiting for the other surgeons to complete their part of the procedure. With Chloe, everything was going extremely well, which put me slightly on edge.

Every physician dreads giving the families of their charges bad news, but the angst I felt at the possibility of giving Stephanie Barker bad news about her child, wasn't my version of normal. While my eyes alternated between the vital sign readouts and the monitors displaying Dr. Maxwell's progress with restoring Chloe's still child-like face to its formerly unblemished state, my thoughts drifted back to the woman who'd stolen my breath with a mere glance.

While we'd worked together to restore function to Chloe's lungs, and once I was sure she was out of danger, I'd pumped Pearson for whatever information he had on the stunning Stephanie Barker. All under the guise of gaining a clear picture of the patient and any potential dangers. Pearson seemed none the wiser. As medical professionals, we were required to report any suspected child abuse to the authorities. I didn't for a second think Stephanie would hurt the angelic looking pre-teen, but I needed a plausible reason to ask questions.

Turns out Pearson didn't know much other than Stephanie was Chloe's aunt by familial ties, but was legally her adoptive mother. The child had been brought to the hospital in an ambulance, accompanied by a woman who claimed to be her mother. Pearson relayed the tense interaction between the two women and a large man whose name he didn't know. As much as I wanted to know about the unknown man, I didn't press.

"Ok Sweet Pea, we're all done now. Scar or no scar, you're beautiful, but I made sure you won't have to re-live this day every time you look in the mirror." Dr. Maxwell's soft voice pulled me from my thoughts to refocus on what was taking place in the operating room. No one commented on the doctor speaking to the patient as if she was fully conscious and could hear. It was Georgina's thing.

Giving instructions to the techs, Georgina and I removed the protective gear as we exited the OR. We left Pearson and Georgina's resident behind to make sure our orders were carried out as instructed. In silent consensus we turned towards the elevators to take us to the waiting area to speak to the family.

"Not that I mind the company, but you want to fill me in on what's going on to make you hang around the OR an extra hour watching me work?"

I should have known she would call me out. Georgina and I were among the handful of Asians on the surgical staff at Talbot, so we'd become friendly over the years. Nothing romantic, I wasn't her type and we were colleagues, so I wouldn't cross that line even if I were. Besides, she was married.

Me being Chinese American and her being from the Philippines gave us a sort of kinship in an environment where we rarely saw peers who looked like us. There were more than a few Asian doctors and nurses, but not in the surgical group. The surgical group was predominantly white and male. Talbot Memorial had a very ethnically diverse staff, but the number of white males in the higher-end fields still eclipsed the other minority groups.

Brushing off Georgina's comment about the extra attention I gave the patient, I answered, "I just thought it would be better if we spoke to the family together. I've only met the mother, Stephanie Barker, and she was pretty shaken up. From what I heard, Chloe was the victim of a vicious attack. I had a feeling if I went in to update her and couldn't give her the whole story, it wouldn't go over well."

Try as I might to project a professional tone and demeanor, I wasn't sure it worked. She knew me too well. We'd even double dated a couple of times when I'd actually had a significant other.

"Uh-huh. That's what you're going with?" She regarded me shrewdly. "Ok. I'll allow it. *For now*," she conceded as we exited the elevator and walked towards the double doors leading away from the surgical suites.

As we drew nearer to the waiting area, I heard raised voices. Shooting a quick glance at Georgina, I picked up my pace. It's normal for tensions to run high when a loved one has to undergo surgery. Instinct was telling me our patient's family was the source of the noise and the possibility of Stephanie being subjected to any more distress didn't sit well with me. Not in the least.

Rounding the corner into the waiting area, my eyes surveyed the room in one sweeping glance. There were four people in the waiting area. Stephanie was the only person I recognized. Standing with her were a pretty African American woman and a tall, muscular African American man. Sitting a short distance away, separated from the others by body language and low padded benches, was another very pretty African American woman. There was a slight resemblance between the woman seated and Stephanie. A relative? I didn't know and wouldn't ask.

The seated woman had her arms folded across her chest, and her face set in a stubborn expression. When we'd entered the space, there was dead silence—a complete contrast to what we'd heard as we walked towards the waiting room.

"Don't you dare sit there looking at me like I'm stupid. I know you know who it was!" Stephanie's voice barked out into the silence, directed at the seated woman.

Turning her face to the television mounted on the wall, the woman snapped back, "I already told you I don't know nothin'."

Everything after her statement happened at lightning speed. Stephanie took two steps and launched herself over the low bench, landing on her feet directly in the space in front of the seated woman. I didn't wait to see if the others would try to stop her as I hurried over to diffuse the situation.

I wasn't quick enough to stop her from landing a closed-hand blow to the woman's face knocking her head into the wall behind her. *Shit!* That looked like it hurt like hell. The woman cried out grabbing her cheek with one hand and the back of her head with the other.

Wrapping my arms around Stephanie, trapping her arms to her sides, I bodily moved her away from the woman, while she kicked out making threats. If the other woman made any attempts to fight back, I didn't notice.

"Let me go Gene! I'm going to stomp a mudhole in that stupid, selfish, bitch's ass!" She ground out.

Placing my face next to hers, I spoke lowly, directly into her ear, "I'm not Gene. I'm Jian and I need you to stop struggling, Sweetheart."

Her body went completely still in my embrace. Relieved, I exhaled deeply. For a moment, I was concerned her anger wouldn't allow her to hear anyone else.

Continuing in a low, hopefully calming, voice, I encouraged her. "That's it."

My chest was pressed into her back and I could feel her heart still thumping rapidly. Keeping her snuggled against me, her feet barely touching the floor, I worked to calm her.

"Breathe... In... Out... Just like that...It's not going to help your little girl if security has to escort you out of the hospital."

The breathing exercise helped, but my last statement seemed to really do the work to get her body to completely relax. Her heart rate was still quick, but I felt the beats slowing. My mind could have been playing tricks on me, but the pulsations seemed to slow until they matched my own.

Pushing the thought away, I gently placed her on her feet and slowly released her from my arms. Raising to my full height, I moved until I was standing in front of her, obscuring her view of the woman silently seething in the chair.

Ignoring the other people in the room, I captured her hands with mine, probing her dark eyes with my own. Silently, we assessed one another. I couldn't say what conclusion she reached, but her face softened before she tugged lightly, trying to remove her hands from mine. Grudgingly, I allowed it.

"Thank you," she said softly, her eyes drifting away from mine to notice Georgina's presence in the room. I quickly made introductions between the two. In turn, she introduced me and Georgina to the man and the other woman in the room. She blatantly refused to acknowledge the seated woman. The man was introduced as her cousin Gene and the woman as her friend Joy.

My relief in hearing the man was a relative was enough to make me want to break out in my happy dance. Since it wasn't a possibility at the moment, I danced on the inside. *Why?* The reason's not important.

Motioning to a grouping of chairs on the other side of the room, Georgina and I ushered them over to relay the outcome of the procedures. I managed to stop myself from gathering her back into my arms when Stephanie teared up upon hearing Chloe, who she called Saffi, would most likely make a full recovery with minimal, if any, scarring to her face as a result.

Unable to resist, I placed a hand atop the hand she rested on her own thigh, "Chloe will be in recovery for another hour or so, then we'll move her to room. She'll need to stay here for another couple of days for us to monitor the situation with her lungs to be certain she won't require further intervention. As soon as she's assigned a room, someone will let you know."

"Thank you, Dr. Anderson. Thank you too, Dr. Maxwell," her honeyed voice was tinged with the scratchy remnants of closely held emotions.

"You're welcome. We're happy to do what we can to help," Georgina responded, getting to her feet. I could feel her eyes boring into the side of my head. Reluctantly, I released Stephanie's hand and stood alongside Georgina.

As we were preparing to make our exit, two uniformed police officers entered the waiting room, visually scanning everyone present. The older of the two spoke for the duo, "Excuse us, we're looking for the parents or guardians of a Chloe Barker."

My eyes shot to Stephanie's face and my body went rigid. Georgina tugged at my sleeve to get my attention. She whispered, "I think we should go now." I was loath to leave, but I knew I had no real reason to remain behind. Outside of performing the procedure to repair Chloe's lung, I had no ties to her nor Stephanie. *So why can't I walk away?*

Slowly, I turned and started to follow Georgina from the room. As we left, I took mental note of the officer's names. Memorizing them, I flicked one more reassuring glance in Stephanie's direction. Instead of catching her eyes, I caught the expression on her cousin's face. His facial countenance was neutral, but his eyes were probing mine.

For a short moment, we stood this way, speaking without words. Finally, he dipped his head in an almost imperceptible nod before placing his eyes on the officers speaking to Stephanie. Nothing left to say or do, I left the room, trailing behind my colleague.

After we made it to the elevator, Georgina spoke again, "You know you're eventually going to have to tell me what's up right?" Not hearing a response from me, she continued into the elevator and pressed to button for her floor.

I wasn't ready to talk to anyone about my actions because I needed time to figure out what was going on myself. I'm not a eunuch, but I've never had my attraction to anyone be so instant and all-consuming that it took a concerted effort for me to remain detached and professional. If I were being completely truthful with myself, I didn't succeed at remaining detached. I failed at that one. *Big time.*

Contact the author.

I'd love to stay connected with you! Visit my website for more information and sign up for my newsletter.
https://dariemccoyllc.com

Connect with me on Social Media!
https://www.tiktok.com/@dariemccoy
https://www.instagram.com/authordarie
https://www.facebook.com/darie.mccoy

www.ingramcontent.com/pod-product-compliance
Lightning Source LLC
Chambersburg PA
CBHW051303170626
46809CB00004B/1756